I0744266

Hayes

RETRIBUTION KINGS BOOK 3

ELLA MILES

Copyright © 2023 by Ella Miles

EllaMiles.com

Ella@ellamiles.com

Cover design © CBC Designs / Designs by Daqri

All rights reserved.

No part of this book may be reproduced in any form or by any electronic or mechanical means, including information storage and retrieval systems, without written permission from the author, except for the use of brief quotations in a book review.

Retribution Kings Series

Lennox (Book 1)
Rialta (Book 2)

Hayes (Book 3)
Lilith (Book 4)

Gage (Book 5)
Nova (Book 6)

The Retribution Kings Series is a spinoff of the Retribution Games Series. If you want to read Beckett and River's story, start with Mistaken Hero

CHAPTER 1

Hayes

ALL EYES SNAP to me as Gage and I step into the ballroom. It's an uneasy feeling seeing half the room looking at me with hate-filled eyes, while the other half looks at me with lust-filled eyes. Dead or in their bed—the room's wishes for me are split down the middle.

Only a small handful of people in this room are actually my friends. But more are warming up to me every day since we first came back to the Retribution Kings six months ago.

It was a risk. We knew we could have been killed on the spot. We were enemies, and Retribution Kings are good at one thing—revenge.

And yet we took the chance, knowing our mission is more important than our lives. It helped that the Retribution Kings were still in disarray and hadn't chosen a new leader yet. So after enduring some brutal trials, Gage and I were reinstated as Retribution Kings. The only thing Retribution Kings enjoy almost as much as retribution is a good celebration.

All the judgmental eyes on me should put me in my place, but I thrive on the attention.

I widen my grin, knowing that even the men here who hate me can't touch me now that I'm one of them. I let my eyes rake through the room, pausing on the eyes of the women who look at me like they want to devour me.

Gage rolls his eyes. Despite being in the same position as me, no one looks at him. He's security. He's good at blending into the shadows—a skill he's mastered. For a moment, I envy him. It must be nice to carry out your duties without an audience. But then, *what fun is that?*

I look back at him, but he's already gone.

I'm on my own.

No, that's not true. Gage will be watching me. He's always with me. He's one of my best friends. I'm never alone.

I adjust the black tie of my suit as I lick my lips—feeling more heated stares. It's time to go to work.

I step out onto the wooden dance floor. No sooner does my foot hit the floor am I crowded by women. They flock to me. When they see me, they don't see a threat. They see a man with thick muscles, piercing green eyes beneath sharp glasses, and long hair to run their hands through. They see a bad boy who isn't really that bad. They see my charming smile and jovial laugh, and they can't help but smile themselves. They know I'm fun. I'm a pleaser in bed, and I'd be the best fuck of their lives.

"Hayes, it's so good to see you here," the woman hanging off my right arm says. I should know her, I might've even fucked her, but I can't remember her name.

"You look dashing in a tux," another says.

"Dance with me," the boldest says.

I can barely move without knocking them all over. So I do what I always do—I grin and let my eyes smolder for each of them. I look at each one as if she is the only person in this room I'd like to fuck, when really I'm here for a much more important mission. I can't get distracted, not tonight.

"Hayes, come with me," Titus Adler says.

The women part, letting Titus, the newly appointed Retribution Kings leader, through.

"Ladies," I say before I step through them to follow Titus. When we are well enough away from them, I say, "Thank you."

Titus chuckles, glancing back at the women still swooning after me.

"I admit, I don't get why the ladies flock to you. You're not that good-looking; you haven't even bothered to get a haircut," Titus teases as he stands in his sharp tux. It molds to his body perfectly, complementing his thick black hair. He's a good-looking man as well. I'm surprised more women aren't surrounding him, especially now that he's the leader.

"And your hair is far too short and choppy for anyone woman to find you attractive," I tease back.

Titus grips my shoulder. "It's good to see you, old friend."

I raise my brows. "It's good that you still consider me your friend after everything. Most here think I deserve a bullet to the head."

Titus motions to a waiter, who brings over a tray of drinks. Titus removes two scotches and hands one to me.

"You've proven yourself, Hayes. Which is why I want to offer you a position."

I lift the drink to my lips as I feel more stares on us from the crowd. All of them are wondering why Titus is giving me so much attention at the party celebrating his new leadership. I'm curious about the same thing.

"I want to offer you the position as my second."

My mouth falls open as my eyes shoot wide. There's no hiding my shock.

"Your second? But what about Mackenzie, Cooper, or even…"

"No, I don't trust any of them. Not with the Retribution Kings. Not with my life."

I frown. "But I've already betrayed the Retribution Kings before. No one trusts me."

"Exactly, no one can bribe you. The only man here you'd put before me is Gage—and he's good at security."

"Which is why if you were to offer either of us the position, you should offer it to Gage. He's much better at gathering intel and keeping others safe." I should know since that's what he's currently doing.

"Yea, he's good at that, and I'm sure he's listening in on this conversation at this very moment. And I need him too. I need him protecting the Retribution Kings. I need him securing our borders and protecting our people. He's already accepted the job as my head of security."

I raise a brow as Titus continues.

"My second is public-facing. He's the man people talk to before they talk to me. I need a man who can charm anyone. Someone who can spy on anyone while standing right next to them and them none the wiser. A man who can put anyone at ease, while he persuades them to my causes."

I take another sip, giving me a second to prepare my reply. "I can't charm anyone that doesn't already want to be charmed. You can feel the looks in the crowd. Most of the men here hate me."

"And yet, you're not dead. Why do you think that is?" He cocks his head, looking at me like he already knows the answer. It's why he chose me.

I swallow. "I don't think I'm the best man for the job."

"Except you are. You've played second to others before, to Lennox—"

"And look how that turned out. I'm his enemy now."

"Yea, okay." Titus stops talking and lets a heavy pause pass between us as he looks out at the crowd. Together we scan the women in beautiful dresses and men in fine tuxes, all here to celebrate him.

"I'll consider your offer," I tell him.

His lips turn up. "Good. I'm not offering the job to anyone else."

I swallow hard. Titus and I go way back. We used to be friends, but he was never part of our circle. He never thought he'd be the leader, never thought he'd have a chance at power.

Despite that, or maybe because of that, I think Titus will be a good leader. But I'm not sure if I can trust him yet.

The eyes of the crowd burn into us, so I do what I always do. I grin like I love basking in the attention. Then I wink at the nearby sexy woman in the too-tight black dress, one of many vying for my attention.

Titus chuckles. "Say yes."

"What?"

"Be my second. I don't know how you do it, but with one fucking grin, every woman's panties are drenched with desire for you. And several of the men can't help themselves; their lips are lifting."

"You don't need me to get anyone to like you. You won the leadership. Everyone already likes you."

Titus shakes his head. "I may have won and become the leader, but that doesn't mean everyone likes me. Our group is divided after everything that's happened. At some point, I'll make a decision that will piss some faction off. And that's why I need you. You can enchant anyone."

"You put too much faith in me."

"Maybe, but there is no one else better. I trust you."

"You shouldn't. You're the leader of the Retribution

Kings—the only way you stay the leader is if you trust no one."

"Or if I trust the right people."

I take a deep breath, already knowing what my decision will be. It's why I came back. Having Titus's trust and some of his power will help us complete our mission faster than we thought.

"I'll be your second," I sigh.

Titus's face lights up as he holds his hand out to me, and I shake his hand, sealing my fate.

Hunter walks over before we can discuss anything further. "It's time for your speech."

Titus nods and turns toward the stage.

I follow after, already knowing where my place is.

Titus glances to me with a knowing smile, thrilled to have me in the job.

My chest seizes. I hope I can be loyal to him, but I'll always be loyal to my friends above everything else. He knows that, but he thinks my friendship extends to him.

We walk to the stage, and I follow like a shadow. Even though Gage is now head of security, in charge of keeping the crowd safe, I'm in charge of keeping Titus safe.

Titus begins speaking, and the crowd listens. The room hangs onto his every word. He's wrong to think he needs a man like me to help him. But now that I've accepted the job, I'm not going to argue.

I stare out into the crowd, holding the gaze of each person individually. I try to put them all at ease, working my charm from a distance. But I'm also working on my own mission—to find one woman in particular who holds the secrets to getting my friends our own retribution. I search, not really sure what I'm looking for as I have no idea what she looks like. I only know her name.

My heart stops as my gaze falls on a pair of glistening

green eyes. My breath is swept away from the pull of those eyes. Eyes I try to move on from, but her stare yanks me to her like a summons I can't escape.

I feel like I've been punched in the gut and hit over the head with the impact of her look.

I stumble back a step, almost falling off balance, before regaining my composure. I'm sure those watching me think I've lost it if I can't even stand behind Titus without almost falling over.

Smiling for the crowd, I try to keep the facade up.

But my gaze is locked on the woman with the green eyes that penetrate through me like a knife through butter. I notice more about her now—fiery red curls, thick lips, and a glittering dress that matches the shade of her green eyes. I've never seen her before. I don't know who she is. *Is she a Retribution King? Married to one? An outsider?*

Titus finishes his speech, and I force myself to follow him off the stage, losing my direct line of vision to her.

"What's wrong? It looks like you've seen a ghost," Titus says.

"Who is that woman?" I ask, pointing to her in the crowd.

"That's Ruby West."

My head snaps to him. *It can't be.* My lips curl up in a wicked smile. *Finally, fate is on my side.*

Titus chuckles. "Enjoy your night. Tomorrow your duties start. But tonight is yours to enjoy as you please."

I nod, snapping my eyes back to Ruby. I know exactly how I plan on enjoying my night.

CHAPTER 2

Hayes

RUBY TURNS AND WALKS AWAY, her emerald dress swishing with every step she takes. My eyes fall on the elegant lines of her subtle back muscles and then down to the curve of her hips that sway back and forth. I have to remind myself that I need to study all of her to take my eyes off her ass. I force my gaze to the bounce of her red ringlets of hair that she sweeps to one side as I get flashes of her delicate neck.

Everything about her draws me to her. The way she looks and walks, sure, but her pull on me is so much more than that. It's the like there's a glow around her I can't look away from—I have to follow. Even if she wasn't my mission, I'd follow her.

I don't understand this draw to her. I'm a playboy, a womanizer. I've bedded more women than I can count. I'm known for bringing women pleasure and not worrying about my own. I've never felt like this before with any woman, especially one I haven't even touched or talked to.

I'm only drawn to her because my instincts are screaming at me that she's the one who can solve the mystery that took everything from us. And once I get her to talk to me, she'll go back to being just a woman. At least, that's what I tell myself as I follow her like she's cast a spell on me.

She walks through the crowd, talking to no one. Maybe she knows I'm following her, so she's leading me somewhere private.

But that can't be. She doesn't know who I am.

She walks confidently through the ballroom doors and then down the hallway toward the exit.

I jog to catch up to her, slamming my hand on the door to keep her from escaping before I can work my allure on her. My breath is hot on her neck, and as I breathe in her sweet scent akin to warm sugary vanilla, an explosion of desire burns through my body. My cock is straining against my zipper, and I haven't even touched her yet. She has no idea how turned on I am. No clue that I'm losing my fucking mind over her, even though I have no idea who she really is or why I'm having this strong of a reaction to her.

Ruby doesn't turn around. Her breath catches in her throat. She feels my presence—the undeniable tug between us. She senses the purr of electricity swirling swiftly through the air around us.

"Who are you?" I breathe out, even though I already know her name. And because I know her name—I know some of her background. I know she's the daughter of a wealthy Retribution King. I know she's engaged to be married to Samson Evans. I know she's grown up in this world, and therefore, she's survived great trauma. We all have to have made it to young adulthood and still belong to the Retribution Kings. I don't know what exactly she endured during her initiation, just that she's a survivor like all of us. But my words spill out, needing to know the truth of her. *Why am I so drawn to her? Who is she really? What are her real desires? Does she really want to marry Samson, or is it an arranged marriage?*

"You already know my name; it's why you came looking for me." Her words shock me, but I don't let her know that.

"Yes, but I want more than your name. Who are you?"

She doesn't answer me. There is no way to answer my question with a simple sentence.

I suck in a breath, gulping down more of her scent—getting whiffs of a crisp, citrusy aura this time. My body aches with more need for her from each additional breath. It's terrifying how quickly my body reacts to her.

I'm turned on by plenty of women, but never this fast and never with this much intensity.

"You're the most beautiful woman I've ever seen."

She huffs, turning and facing me. "Really? That's your pickup line? The most beautiful woman you've ever seen? How many times have you used that tonight alone? I've seen you with the other women. Some women may find your cocky arrogance attractive, but you're going to have to work harder with me."

I grin wider than I've ever grinned before, and my eyes shine brightly with thick desire.

"None, and I don't mind a little extra work. You're the most intoxicatingly beautiful woman with the sharpest mouth I've ever met."

"I doubt that, sunshine."

"Sunshine? I like that."

"I don't. I hate the sun. It tricks you into thinking you're happy with its vitamin D and sunny disposition. It's only later that you realize it burned your skin and gave you cancer."

"I won't hurt you."

"You will. All men hurt."

She's been hurt. *Betrayed? Abused? Raped?* I don't know

where her trauma comes from—just that I can see it in her eyes. There's a dullness now where I saw the sparkle earlier.

Still, I can't stop beaming at her. I can't stop wanting her. It's like I found something I didn't know I was searching for—I can't explain it. I don't know this woman any more than she knows me. She's beautiful, but there are plenty of beautiful women here tonight. It's something else, something deeper. Something yanks me to her, something beyond the real reason I came here tonight.

"And yet, you still want me."

Her eyes widen at my blazed words. "You are cocky...and wrong."

"I'm not." My eyes drag down her body in a heated glaze. "Your pulse is quickening in your neck. You haven't swallowed in over a minute, and when you do again, it will be a hard swallow, pushing down your own thirst for me. Your lips are parted, practically begging to be kissed. Your nipples have hardened beneath your dress—I can see their peaks through the thin material. And I'm guessing your panties, if you're wearing any, have a damp spot of arousal marked on them."

She shakes her head. "You're so fucking wrong. You think you caused all of that in me by just coming after me. By putting your burly arm in front of me, preventing me from leaving, and flashing me one smug smirk, my panties are melting off. You think I'd spread my legs for you in the nearest cheap hotel room. You're full of yourself if you actually think that."

"Why? It's true."

"Just because other women find you attractive doesn't mean I do. Your hair is too long, your glasses are too big, you should shave that scruff off your face, and you grin far too often for any one of them to be genuine." Her eyes narrow in on my dimple, and her mouth runs dry. She licks her lips, moistening them. "Any man who walks around like he's god's gift to women is an asshole, and not a man I'd ever consider fucking."

I shudder in delight at her tongue lashing. *Is this love? Is this true desire?* There's a throbbing in my chest as I cling to her every word. I want to know all of her thoughts. I want to know everything.

"Stop grinning at me. It's annoying," she quips.

"It's who I am. I can't help it any more than you can help being surely."

"I'm not surely."

"You are."

"I just don't want to fuck a playboy."

My grin softens as I pause a moment, taking a step back.

"Giving up so easily?" she smirks.

"I'd never give up on you." My voice drops in pitch, and my lips straighten out.

"Then you're a fool."

"Come with me." I hold out my hand to her.

"Why would I ever come with you?"

Suddenly, voices begin echoing through the hallway, and I know I'm about out of time. I'm going to have to up my appeal to get her to leave with me.

Usually, I just bat my eyes and grin, and women are putty in my hands. If that doesn't work, I cook for them. Women can't resist a man who can cook. And if that doesn't work, I tell them about my Prince Albert piercing on my cock that none of them have been able to resist taking a ride on.

I don't have time for any of that. And I'm not sure any of my usual tricks would work with Ruby.

Her pupils dilate as she glances behind me, and I finally get a small clue about her. I see a way to get her to leave with me.

"You're hiding from someone, and I have a car parked at the entrance that I can help you escape in."

The voices grow closer.

She grits her teeth together, like it pains her to make this decision.

"Fine," she says.

I grab her hand and push her out the front door. Her fingers intertwine with mine in the most natural way, like the missing piece of my puzzle. She fits me perfectly.

Fuck, I can't fall for her. Ruby is the last person I should start a relationship with. She's just my mark, nothing more.

We make it twenty feet down the path when the doors behind us open, and voices carry outside. My car is more than a hundred feet in front of us. Her hand grows clammy in mine, and she begins to shake.

"We're not going to make it to your car," she says.

My brows pinch together, and we walk faster. I was wrong. Clearly, whoever she's hiding from is a bigger threat than I first realized.

"We're almost there," I say, trying to reassure her.

Her eyes are wild as she searches in the darkness for safety. She doesn't realize that by holding my hand, she's as safe as she could possibly be. I feel an instant need to protect this woman—even from myself.

If the person she's running from were to fire a bullet at her, I'd take it for her. I don't know why. I don't know what my fascination is with her, but I'm hers. I can barely even remember my mission. I no longer care to fuck her to piss off her soon-to-be husband or father. Or to get information from her. All I want is her for myself.

"We aren't going to make it," she whispers, her voice trembling.

My eyes narrow at her as I start to break out into a run. I didn't take her as a woman that would give up so easily or be so terrified of anyone. She has a shield around her that I mistook for resilience. I thought she's been hardened to the realities of the world, but this woman is desperately afraid of something or someone.

Suddenly, she halts to a stop, yanking my arm back.

My eyes widen, and my jaw falls open to tell her we can make it.

Looking at her now, there's the determination back in all of her features that I saw before.

"Please." Her teeth rake over her bottom lip.

"Anything." I let my body go slack, and she pulls me hard to her body at the edge of the sidewalk.

She takes a deep breath and then throws herself at me. Her arms pull my head to hers, and then her lips crash against mine in a strangled kiss.

I'm so caught off guard that I stumble into her, my lips pressed against hers but not moving. Her tongue lashes against mine, begging me for entrance into my mouth. I accept the invitation easily and thrust my tongue into her slick mouth.

My body hardens as I finally start kissing her back. She's heaven in my mouth. Her tongue doesn't hold back—this isn't a kiss she's giving because she's using it as a distraction or a way to hide. This kiss is pure us, exactly how a first kiss should be.

Her hot tongue continues to explore my mouth as I press my broad body against her small curves. I walk her backward until her back hits the trunk of a willow tree. And then I bunch her dress up at her hip, needing to feel her.

I want to ravish every part of her. I want to undress her slowly, take my time peeling every piece of clothing off of her, and then fuck her like she's never going to be fucked again.

We shouldn't fuck here. Even under these willow tree

branches, we aren't completely hidden away. But if I don't have her soon, I'm afraid we'll both die. I've never felt this strong of an urge before, never been so consumed by a woman.

This has to be a dream. It can't be real, this feeling.

Ruby pulls back a second, breaking the seal between our lips. Her eyes are hooded as she stares down at my mouth, and her fingers brush over her lips. She's just as affected as I am.

Slowly, her eyes lift to mine, and there's a flicker of fear. She's afraid of this feeling.

I nod, unable to speak or tell her I feel the fucking same, but there is nothing we can do to stop this feeling now.

I lower my lips to hers and gently nudge her lips apart again. My mouth tests to see if the electricity is still there.

I gasp as our lips touch, and the shock returns to both of us.

Jesus fucking Christ. What spell has this woman cast on us?

Suddenly, I hear a female voice but don't make out who it is or what the woman is saying.

Ruby places her hand on my chest but doesn't stop kissing me. It's like she can't.

And yet, I can feel her slipping. Her brain is returning to its normal state, which means her common sense is going to return, and she's going to end this.

I curve my hands over her ass, tilting her body to me so she can feel how turned on I am, how much I want her. If she leaves now, I'm not going to let this go. I'm going to hunt her down until we both fuck this feeling out of us.

An audible swallow leaves her throat at the sound of the woman behind us calling out again. Ruby shoves me hard this time, severing the connection between us.

My eyes train on her as she runs out from under the

willow tree and back to the sidewalk, where she meets a woman in a plain black dress.

Ruby wraps her arms around this woman in a hug.

Can the young woman smell me on Ruby? Does she know what we were doing? Can she tell that Ruby's mine?

Ruby's eyes cut back to where I'm standing for the briefest of seconds, and I swear I see longing in her eyes.

Don't worry, surely one. You won't have to wait long to have me—all of me.

Ruby pulls the woman under her arm, and she starts walking down the path with her, away from me.

I wait a moment longer and walk out from under the branches and back to the path, trying to decide if I'm leaving or if I should find Titus or Gage. I don't have to do either, as Titus finds me.

"That's Lilith Hart, and her younger sister," Titus says.

My heart slams to a stop.

"What? I thought you said that was Ruby West?"

Titus shakes his head. "Sorry, I thought you were pointing to the woman to her left."

Oh, fuck. The woman I kissed, the woman I nearly fucked against a tree, the woman I'm madly in love with, isn't the woman I need to find.

Lilith is no one to me. She's a distraction that will keep me from completing my mission. She's an innocent who doesn't belong in my world.

I have to stay away.

I can't drag her down with me.

Lilith doesn't deserve it.

I have to find Ruby, not Lilith. I have to let Lilith go, no matter how impossible that will be.

And then I look at Titus, and my heart sinks. He's staring after Lilith with lust in his eyes. I know that gaze all too well because it was the gaze I had until I found out who she is.

"I'm going to make Lilith Hart the queen to my king. And I need your help," Titus says.

My eyes stare into the darkness, and I don't speak. *What is there to say?* He clearly didn't see me with her. He doesn't know I claimed her first. If either of us cares about her, then she doesn't belong with either of us. The best way to keep her safe is to keep her away from me.

I don't say any of those things. I can't. I agreed to be his second, and I'm going to need his trust to protect those I care about. So I have no choice but to accept my fate.

Fate has always been cruel to me. It's why I don't let myself fall in love. And this feeling I have for Lilith, it can't be love. It has to just be infatuation and lust, nothing more.

That's a lie.

But I'll keep lying to myself forever if I have to.

Fate has decided I should suffer for loving Lilith, for loving what's not mine.

CHAPTER 3

Lilith

"GO TO SLEEP," I say, standing at the doorway to my sisters' room. "I mean it. Don't stay up all night watching movies, Kennedy."

She just rolls her eyes at me. "It's Saturday night. We have nowhere to be in the morning, so we can sleep in. It doesn't matter if we stay up all night or not."

Kennedy moves her blankets aside for Adeline to jump into bed with her, smiling in agreement.

I sigh. They have nowhere important to be tomorrow, but I do. Tomorrow our lives change forever. No more living in this shitty trailer with its busted furnace, leaky water heater, and flimsy siding the wind bursts through. No more scraping by for enough money to buy stale bread and canned soup. No more worrying.

Kennedy's right though—there is no reason for them not to stay up all night being teenagers. At seventeen, Kennedy only has one more year left before initiation. I only have one year to prevent her from having to endure that fate.

Thankfully, Adeline, at only thirteen, has several years

before she has to worry about the truth of the dangerous organization we belong to.

I flick off the lights to their room as the glow from Kennedy's tablet fills the room.

"Thank you for letting me come with you tonight. I had fun dancing," Kennedy says.

I nod.

I didn't want to bring her, but she begged, and there was only so much I could do to keep her from coming. If I didn't let her come, she'd only sneak in this time or the next.

"Come watch movies all night with us," Kennedy says suddenly.

"Yea, there's plenty of room for you, Mom," Adeline says.

My heart seizes. She doesn't call me mom often anymore, but every once in a while, Adeline slips even though we haven't seen our real mom in weeks. She's always working, doing whatever she can to bring us enough money to survive—including selling herself to men at night to keep the lights on here.

That level of desperation is something I'm going to put a stop to. Adeline deserves a chance to know our mother. I'm not a good replacement. Our mother is a saint. She's kind and funny and warm. But after our father died, she threw herself into providing for us. She's trying to get us out from underneath the Retribution Kings, but nothing she's done has made a dent in the debts we owe them.

But I've found a way to save us all.

I yawn. I don't have to fake it; I'm exhausted. "Sorry, I'm too old and too tired to stay up."

Adeline sighs.

Kennedy narrows her eyes at me as if she can see through my lies.

"Sleep tight," I say and shut the door before either can

start questioning me. I haven't told them my plan, and I don't intend to. They never need to know what I'm going to do to save them, to keep them innocent and untouched and free.

I head to the bedroom I share with Mom, which means it's practically my own room since she's never here. There are two full beds in here, each sitting on a cheap metal bed frame. No headboard. No comforters. No decorative pillows. *Why would we spend money on such frivolous things?*

The walls are a light shade of yellow from whoever lived here before. My skin crawls at the sight of the pastel shade every time—it's far too happy of a color. The only personalized things in the room are a borrowed library book on astrology that I read before bed and a dirty coffee mug next to Mom's bed. If I leave her things untouched, it's like she just left for work this morning. It means she'll return, and I can pretend she's not actually in some Retribution King's bed—fucking him for enough money to feed her daughters.

Soon, Mother, soon.

I've already changed out of my slinky dress and into a tank top and shorts. The dress is hanging over the door to the closet, to be returned to my friend Abigail in the morning. There is no way I could afford a dress like that on my own.

As I slide into bed, I plan on reading more of my book. I flip the first page open, but instead of focusing on the words on the page, all I can think about is *him*.

The mysterious stranger from tonight with the bright green eyes, long dark hair pulled into a bun, and full-framed glasses. He was a shameless flirt, but he'd helped me escape talking to Farrah. I wasn't afraid to talk to her. I was afraid of what I would do to her if I was alone with her after she stole Kennedy's phone and smashed it. It would take us months to earn enough money to buy her a new phone if I didn't already have my plan in place. Right now, I really can't go to prison. My family needs me too much.

I close my book and shut my eyes, hoping sleep will quickly take me. But the feel of his lips on mine takes control of my body. My lips still feel swollen from his bruising kisses, and my body hums with the feeling of his touch.

I don't know his name or who he is. I do know he's Titus's second in command—that was clear from the way he was standing at Titus's side—but any more than that is lost on me.

All I know is the connection I felt to him. My body wanted him even when my mind was screaming for me to run away from him. He's not in the plan, and being with him would ruin everything. And I have no plan B, only plan A.

A wildfire spreads through my body, and a familiar ache surges between my legs. I shift uncomfortably in bed, trying to dull the ache. But his damn grin flashes in my head with his adorable dimples, and the ache strengthens.

His grin.

I've never been attracted to a man's smile before, but his almost made this cynical heart want to smile along with him. I couldn't take my eyes off his lips or the little dimple that formed on the side of his cheek.

God, how I wanted him tonight. I'm thankful to Kennedy for calling me before I took things too far. I almost let one night with a complete stranger ruin all of my plans.

I throw the covers over me, trying to block him out. *Sleep, I need sleep, not him.* The heat is still there, but I refuse to touch myself and bring myself any relief. I refuse to give a complete stranger so much power over me.

CHAPTER 4

Lilith

"LILITH HART, I didn't think you'd show," Peter Anderson says.

"I'm here, right on time."

I'm guessing I wouldn't be the first woman who claimed to want his help only to not show up when it came down to it. But I have no choice, so I'm here.

"Come in." He opens the door to his mansion, and I walk into the foyer. My eyes immediately drift up to the three stories towering above me. Each wall is filled with fancy art, a single piece valuable enough to pay for a lifetime of food for our family.

If I wasn't such a bad thief, I'd consider stealing to save my family. But I've tried everything, and this is the only option I have left.

Peter leads me through the first floor of his house to a room at the back.

I keep my eyes down so I don't get angry at all the things he has while my family survives on virtually nothing.

He unlocks a door and motions for me to step inside. When I look up, it's exactly what I'd expect his office to look like. Overly masculine furniture far too big for the space takes up most of the room. Framed diplomas and pictures of his favorite racing cars line the walls. A bookshelf is filled with books that look like they've never been touched.

Peter closes the door and then flips the lock.

I raise an eyebrow but don't say anything. I'm not afraid of him.

He's a large man in his mid-fifties with peppered short hair and stubble on his full face. He's more bulk than muscle per se, but the muscles he does have would be more than enough to overpower me. He could do whatever he wanted to me.

But he won't. I'm not afraid of him.

He stands to make a lot more money with me alive than abused, raped, or dead.

"Have a seat, Lilith."

I take a seat in a leather chair, staring out the window to the garden below his window. I know he's married, and he has two daughters himself. *Does one of them garden? Or is it just for looks like everything else in this house?*

Peter gathers some papers off the desk, and then to my surprise, he pulls his chair around to my side of the desk. He sits in it, coming face to face with me.

I stare down at the papers, my heart pounding.

"I'm going to start this the same way I start all of my conversations—you don't have to do this. I need you to think long and hard about this before you sign. Because once you sign, that's it. You can't back out. Your life will forever be changed."

I cock my head. "I doubt you have this conversation with everyone, only the women who look terrified when they walk in."

"No, I have this conversation with everyone. If you recall

when you initiated, I had this conversation with you then. I do the same with every new initiate, with every person that comes to me for help. I can help, but it always comes with a cost."

I stare into his deep brown eyes and realize he's serious. His tired eyes look like they've seen well beyond his fifty years. He's been doing this job for a long time. I've spoken to him once before when I initiated, but I barely remember that conversation. I remember being terrified then, but I'm not now.

"You're mistaking my anxiety for fear. I'm not afraid of signing those papers. I'm excited. I'm ready. I know this is the right decision."

His eyes bore into me once again, and I swear in this moment, he can see every truth of my life. He can read me like an open book.

Peter nods once, accepting my truth.

"Then read the contract carefully; it can't be changed once you sign it. If you had a lawyer, then I'd suggest they read it too. But you're doing this for money, so I know you don't have one. All I can say is that you can trust me on this. I've been doing this a long time, and I always have the best interests of my clients in mind."

I snort at that, but Peter doesn't respond to my outburst.

I start reading every line of the contract carefully. It feels like a bad dream. This can't be my reality. *How has my life resorted to this?*

Tears well in my eyes, and I'm afraid I'm going to start shaking.

No.

I swallow hard and blink once—forcing the tears back.

I'm not doing this just because I have to. I'm doing this for me. I'm doing this because I'm a Retribution King, and this is what we do—get retribution. And this is the only way I'll get it.

"Pen."

Peter hands me the pen from his desk.

I take it and then lean over his desk, signing my name in one fluid motion on the last line.

"It's done," Peter says, taking the papers from me.

"What's next?"

Peter looks at me curiously, like he sees something in me, but then gently shakes it off.

Weird.

"The bidding starts Friday. I'll arrange everything. All you have to do is show up."

I swallow the lump in my throat. "What if no one else shows up?"

He offers me a knowing smile. "They will."

CHAPTER 5

Lilith

IT'S FRIDAY, and the butterflies in my belly have turned into pterodactyls batting their wings so hard I'm afraid I'm going to throw up. I need to leave now if I'm going to make it to the hotel on time. I stare at myself in the mirror one last time. A red curl has fallen into my eye, and I shake it back.

I don't recognize myself with the makeup and curled hair, even though I'm still in my normal jeans and crop top. But I need to look my best. I need these assholes to empty their bank accounts for me. I'm still not sure that any of them are going to be willing to pay enough for me.

"You look hot," Abigail says.

I look in the mirror, where my best friend stands behind me.

My cheeks blush. I'm not sure I believe her. I've never been considered hot. I've been the ugly duckling for as long as I can remember, always bullied for my too-long legs, nonexistent boobs, and frizzy hair. But I trust my friend. She's the one who did my hair and makeup.

I nod. "It's time."

Her assured smile drops. "You don't have to do this."

Abigail, with her long auburn hair and still-living high-ranking Retribution King father doesn't have to worry about money like I do. She's always had food, clothes, and shelter. She's always had a future. And as an only child, she never had to be responsible for any younger siblings.

"I do. I'm ready."

She sighs as I strut past her, gathering all of my confidence as I leave my bedroom. I'm not going to be that scared, shy girl anymore. This only works if I'm a vixen that everyone wants.

I stop as I enter the living room. "Take care of my sisters. Promise me, Abigail."

"Of course. I promise. But you're the one taking care of them by doing this. And you're still going to be in their lives."

My heart thumps hard in my chest. I wish I could agree with her, but I'm on the way to sell my body to the highest bidder. There's a strong chance that whichever man pays for me won't be letting me see my family much.

I start to turn away, but Abigail throws her arms around me. I can feel her tears wetting my shoulder.

"Let me help you. I have money—"

"No," I say a little too forcibly. "I appreciate it, but no. I've made up my mind."

Abigail nods and lets me go, wiping her tears. I squeeze her hand, trying to reassure her. And then I let go, thankful that my sisters are at school. I'm not sure I would manage a goodbye with them. Abigail will tell them where I went. She'll take care of them.

I open the door, ready to head out to the car Peter sent for me, when I see Mom walking up the cracked sidewalk. Her eyes have circles under them, and she's still wearing her cleaning uniform.

She pauses when she sees me. I don't know how, but she

knows what I'm about to do. I can see it in the way her eyes tighten as she studies me as if for the last time.

She doesn't ask any questions. Peter sent out the invitations two days ago, and I'm sure she came across a copy. I'm not the first woman from this side of town to offer myself up like this, after all.

We both stare at each other, exchanging glances of the women we've become.

I lift my head higher, knowing there is nothing she can say that would stop me from doing this. For one, I've already signed the contract. If I didn't show up or tried to run, Peter would find me.

Mother starts walking. I think she'll embrace me like Abigail did and beg me not to go. She'll tell me she'll take my place or find a way to stop this.

But she does none of those things. As she passes me, she places a hand gently on my shoulder, pausing for the briefest of seconds. Then wordlessly, she walks past me and inside our home.

I exhale a deep breath, knowing I made the right choice. She knows it too. I have to do this to save my family. There is no other way.

CHAPTER 6

Lilith

I WALK into the Waldorf Astoria and feel completely out of place. This is the most expensive hotel I've ever been inside. The few times I've stayed in a hotel, it's usually been a Motel 6.

My eyes pop wide as I take it all in—the crystal chandelier, the marble statues, the fountain out front, and the slick lobby floor with an intricate design. All of it is too much and over the top.

I don't know why Peter chose this hotel. It seems odd for a place to auction off my body, but then maybe no one wanted me. Peter is just going to pamper me with a nice hotel stay this weekend and then send me on my way.

My stomach sinks at that reality. I don't have time to focus on that because the hotel manager is walking toward me. Suddenly I feel like Julia Roberts in Pretty Woman— they know who I am. They know why I'm here, and I'm about to get kicked out of this hotel for the piece of trash I am.

"Ms. Hart? Welcome to the Waldorf Astoria; I'm Jonathan," the man says with a nauseating smile from behind his blue suit. He's got to be mid-thirties with slicked-back black hair, brown eyes, and tanned skin.

"Uh…thank you," I stutter, not understanding how he knew my name. He must have hundreds of guests walk through these doors each day, and I'm a nobody.

"Can I get you a drink? A coffee, maybe? Or water?"

"A water would be good." My heart can't beat any faster than it already is; better stay away from caffeine.

He grins at me before retrieving a water bottle from behind the front desk. I take it from him and stare at the words Avian as they stare back at me. My lips dry.

Jesus, I couldn't even afford the water in this place.

"If you'll follow me, please, I'll show you your room. Your bags have already been brought up."

Room? I almost say, but then remember that Peter said I was to stay here until the auction was over. I assumed it would take the weekend, but he said it would take as long as it takes to ensure I get the most amount of money out of these men.

I nod.

Jonathan starts leading me through the hotel room. I can't believe this is part of his job normally. It's probably just because I look like a person that might try to steal something, some desperate person trying to reset the balance between the rich and the poor. He's only escorting me so the other guests aren't afraid of me.

As we walk, Jonathan talks about the architecture and history of the building, but all the words go in one ear and out the other. My jaw is slack as we walk, and I take in how beautiful the building is—such a mix of what looks like hundreds of years old architecture mixed with the most modern slick designs.

Jonathan just smiles at me the entire time, supposedly undisturbed by the fact I'm in ripped jeans and Converse sneakers. I'm so distracted by everything that I don't even notice the floor we're on until we step off the elevator —the top.

"This way, Ms. Hart." We walk down the hallway to the sole door.

"The penthouse is usually sold as a condo and not a hotel room suite, but as no one is currently renting the place, we agreed to let you use the condo for as long as you require."

I squirm as we stop outside the door, terrified to enter.

"I think you've made a mistake; I—"

"No, there's no mistake. You're Lilith Hart?"

I nod.

He smiles at me knowingly. "Then this is your hotel room. I've been told the guests should start arriving in an hour. You have use of these rooms and a private meal can be arranged for you at any hour of the day or night while you stay here."

And then he opens the door before I have a chance to argue with him more.

I gasp.

He chuckles before covering his mouth, realizing he shouldn't laugh at guests.

"Wow, this is incredible."

"And it's all yours. Four bedrooms. Four bathrooms. A full kitchen. Living room. Dining room. Office. Your bags have been delivered to the master bedroom, which is to your left."

I nod slowly. *This is a dream.*

I swear I hear Jonathan chuckle again at my lack of a response. He explains some more things and then leaves me in the expansive rooms.

I pull my phone out of my pocket and text Peter.

· · ·

Me: They put me in the penthouse. This has to be a mistake. I can't afford this.

I wait a couple of minutes, not touching anything in the room for fear they'll charge me, and I'll spend the rest of my life trying to pay this moment off.

Peter: No mistake. The penthouse allows for the privacy we need. And the fee will be passed along to the final winner.

Me: But then I'll get less money if they have to pay for this suite as well.

Peter: No, trust me. You'll get more because they will understand your value by staying here.

Me: I think you're crazy, and no one is going to show up. I'm not paying for this hotel room if no one shows up. It wasn't in my contract.

Peter: You're not going to have to pay for anything else ever again in your life. Your future husband's money will. I'm about thirty minutes out. I expect you changed into the dress in your closet and presentable by the time I get there.

Me: Yes, Dad...

I start to text that and then stop. He is acting like my

dad. My eyes water, thinking about how much I miss my father and what he would think of me now.

Proud—he'd be proud of me for helping my family. And he'd hate himself for leaving me in this position.

I pocket my phone without texting Peter back and harden my heart. I'm going to need a heart of steel to survive this weekend. I have a job to do, and I'm going to do it without emotion.

I repeat that mantra in my head the entire time I'm getting dressed. Peter arrives with a team of people to set up the penthouse, and I keep repeating my mantra. Man after man strolls into the room—all of them here because of me.

My jaw is slack as I watch the living room of the expansive penthouse fill up. Hiding in the corner in my long, white dress, I somehow feel like a goddess about to be slaughtered by an angry god. The dress has thin straps that cut down in a V between my breasts, barely containing them before flowing out in a long dress that brushes the floor when I walk. I sip a glass of champagne waiters are bringing around, trying to keep my nonchalant composure, but I'm shocked by the number of men that have shown up.

It's just because they like seeing a woman tortured. They don't want to marry me—they just want to fuck me or watch someone else fuck me.

Any doubt of being able to make enough money goes out the window when I see some of the wealthiest Retribution Kings here. These men have so much money that dropping a couple million on me would be like an average person dropping a hundred dollars on a nice dinner. It wouldn't even make a dent in the amount of wealth they have.

Peter walks over to me with a smug smile on his face looking around the crowded room.

I swallow my pride enough to say, "Thank you."

"Don't thank me yet. I've convinced them to show up—we still have to persuade them to spend their money on you." His eyes cut to me. "Although, that won't be a problem in that dress."

I blush and try not to squirm under his gaze. I'm going to have to get used to men looking at me like I'm a property to be bought and paid for soon enough.

"How many more?" I ask, wondering when things are going to get started.

"One."

As he speaks, the last man enters the living room, now clear of furniture to make room for everyone. I can barely see him through the crowd of men in sharp suits, but there is no denying who he is when I see the dark man bun bouncing on top of his head before getting a flash of bold glasses framing his eyes.

"What is *he* doing here?" I ask under my breath. I didn't mean to say the words out loud, but Peter heard me nonetheless.

"Who?" Peter looks out into the crowd. "Oh, Hayes. He's harmless. He always shows at these things. He is a known playboy, after all, but he never does more than participate in the first couple of rounds. He never has the money to buy himself a wife, even if he needs to after what he did to the Retribution Kings."

Peter just laid out a ton of information about the mysterious man I kissed last weekend, but all I heard was that his name is Hayes, and he'll never purchase me. He'll never be my husband.

Hayes's eyes cut through the crowd to me, and he flashes me his signature broad grin—the one that reaches his eyes, forms a dimple on his cheek, and makes my heart skip a beat.

Stupid heart.

Hayes chuckles from across the room, probably because he knows that even from this far away, he can affect me.

He can never be mine, and I can never be his. He's just here for amusement.

And I don't know whether that is the worst kind of torture or relief that I won't end up with a man that actually has an effect on my body. I don't want to marry a man who can control my bodily so easily—and Hayes already knows just how to control my body, mind, and soul.

CHAPTER 7

Hayes

I SEE Lilith standing in the corner of the room next to Peter. She looks like an angry Greek goddess the way she's staring every man down, about to devour them and not in the way that any of them would like. She would eat them all for dinner until there was nothing left of them and then sleep like a baby at night.

Raking my teeth over my bottom lip, I suck in a deep breath at the reason I'm here, especially now that I see her again. The draw to her is just as strong as it was the first time.

I'm totally fucked.

I understand why Lilith Hart is here. I understand why she thinks this is her only option. She's doing it to protect her two younger sisters and to give them a life when she had none. The Retribution Kings demanded everything from her family and didn't protect her when they should have. They don't see her family as innocent. They see them like they see me—a traitor who has repented, someone who cannot be removed from this life but will never be fully accepted ever again.

I wish I could stop this because I know how this game plays out. It will end in the biggest heartbreak imaginable. But there is nothing I can do to save her or me.

So I do what I always do—I grin. I crack jokes. And I pretend that I don't feel any pain.

Peter rattles a butterknife against his glass, causing everyone to hush. There are at least twenty of us here—more than I've ever seen at an event like this. I have my work cut out for me if I'm going to have a chance at winning Lilith.

Winning Lilith—that sentence makes my stomach curl. *She's not a possession.*

Heat flashes in my eyes as she moves, causing her dress to flow and reveal more than I first thought possible. I can see down to her thin white bra and panties beneath the dress. *Fuck, I want to possess her, though.* Forget my talk about her not being property—I want to own her. I want to make her mine. It's misogynistic and wrong, but damn, does Lilith play with my head and make me think things I've never thought about a woman before.

"Thank you all for coming," Peter starts, like we're here for a bbq and not the auction of a woman so her family can get by when any man here could just give her the money without a second thought. It's nothing to them and everything to her.

I don't have the cash unfortunately, otherwise I would do just that. I would give her all my money, even if it ended up creating more problems for me.

Peter continues, and I hold my breath, silently begging her to change her mind. In my mind, I plead for Lilith to put a stop to this before she loses herself completely.

I've seen it before. Others think they're willing to do anything for money. They're already willing to give their bodies and souls in hopes of finding a wealthy husband at the end of this. But they lose themselves in the process. In the end, they almost always beg Peter to get out of their contract.

It doesn't happen to every woman. Some know what they want. They enjoy the attention, the sex, and they are never looking for love. They are happy with the money and to end up married to a powerful Retribution King.

I don't know where Lilith falls. *Will this end up destroying her or make her more powerful than ever?* If it helps her family, I suspect she will never regret it. Her sisters are what matter to her more than anything. I didn't have a lot of time to research her, but her love for her family was clear in every decision Lilith had ever made.

"I know many of you have attended several events like this before, so you understand the rules and how the weekend usually plays out. But this is different." Peter pauses for dramatic effect.

What are you up to, old man?

Peter grins mischievously, proud to reveal his little secret, while Lilith is stoic. She doesn't look surprised or blindsided at all.

So she's in on it.

Of course, she is. I know how Peter operates. Everything is in the contract. It's how he controls the women who agree to this.

Fucking Retribution Kings. If I didn't have issues with them before, I would because of this alone. We should be protecting women—letting them into our ranks, teaching them how to fight, to lead. Instead, we kill their breadwinners and then force them to sell their bodies in order to survive.

Sick.

"Usually, these events only last the weekend, but I suspect this will take a lot longer. I'm not going to put a timeline on it—it will take as long as it takes."

I don't like the sound of this.

"But before I go into the details, I want to introduce to you the woman you all came here for—Lilith Hart."

Peter holds out his hand, and Lilith takes it as he parades her around the room like she's cattle about to be sold at auction.

I study the men in this room. Some already have wives. Some are older than Peter. Some are sick fucks who like to hurt women. Very few would be acceptable for Lilith to be with in any way.

But as she walks around the room, she doesn't show any disgust. She doesn't show any fear. She looks like she's judging all of us, looking down on us as if we're the ones who need her and not the other way around.

And then she walks past me. Her eyes narrow at me with consideration, trying to figure out what I'm doing here.

Trust me, I'm asking myself the same question. This is going to be the ultimate torture for me. She can never be mine. Even if I win her, she won't be mine.

My stomach sinks and twists into tight knots.

Peter stops their circling, ending up back in the same spot they started. I glance around the room and see every man panting at her, determined to make her theirs, at least for one of the auctions.

Bile rises in my throat at how many times I'm going to have to watch her sell different parts of her over and over again, until someone makes a final offer she accepts and becomes their wife or mistress.

I've never seen so many men at an auction like this, never seen so many high ranks in the Retribution Kings. There is no mistake that Lilith is beautiful. If you ask me, she's the most beautiful woman I've ever seen. But them being here has to be more than that. Peter didn't even send a photo around when he sent the invite—as if he knew her name alone was enough to get them to come.

But who is Lilith? What don't I know? And why does my heart already belong to her? Why would I toss her into my car and drive off, hiding with her the rest of our lives, giving up my family, my mission, and my dreams all for her? What is this power she holds over me?

Peter smiles slyly, knowing exactly what he's doing. He's practically salivating at the thought of his huge commission for Lilith's auction.

"As you all know, Lilith has agreed to sell her body over and over until someone makes an offer that is high enough that she agrees to be theirs forever. We offer the tastes of her so you can sample the goods before buying forever."

Sick...sick, sick, sick. I'm not a murderous man. I've killed plenty of times in my life. I'm not afraid of bloodshed, but I usually only kill when others order me to or when the man in question has wronged me. Peter Anderson is going to die for this, and I'm going to be the one to kill him. But I know I'll have to wait for the right time, or I'll ruin everything.

"However, the rules will be slightly different here because Lilith Hart is a virgin."

This isn't the first time we've had a virgin at one of these events. *So why is this different?*

"She's a virgin in all ways. She's never been fucked, brought to orgasm, touched inappropriately, or even kissed. We are going to take our time enjoying her and selling all of her firsts."

Her firsts?!

Fuck me.

But I know it's a lie. I've already stolen her first kiss, and I almost took a whole lot more. Maybe if I did, I could have saved her from this. Now it's too late, and we're both about to pay for my mistake.

CHAPTER 8

Lilith

"SHE'S *a virgin in all ways. She's never been fucked, brought to orgasm, touched inappropriately, or even kissed. We are going to take our time enjoying her and selling all of her firsts."*

Peter's words play in my head. I already knew he would say those words, revealing some of the closest kept secrets of my soul to every man in this room, but I still feel my cheeks blush. After all, I'm a twenty-one-year-old woman, and I'm a virgin. Never been touched. Never been brought to orgasm. Never been fucked. And up until the other night, never even been kissed.

But there hasn't been much time for romance between juggling multiple jobs, planning a way out for my family, and plotting my revenge. It is the Retribution King way to spend your entire life planning revenge, even if you don't succeed or ever accomplish it.

Even if I did have time for romance, until recently, no one has ever looked at me and thought I was beautiful. I've been the ugly duckling that just recently gained her swan wings. My breasts have only recently swelled into something other than a flat chest, my hips have grown into a womanly curve, and my frizzy hair has finally tamed enough to style.

"Prove it? If you expect us to pay more because she's a virgin, then we demand she be examined first," says a middle-aged man with balding hair and a protruding belly so big he probably needs a mirror to see his own cock.

I scowl at him in disgust. It will be my luck that he wins each round, and I'll be stuck giving him all of my firsts.

It doesn't matter. My firsts mean nothing to me—it's just a body. What matters is that my family can eat, and I will be able to get my revenge once I'm won and married to a man in this room.

Peter grabs my chin forcefully.

What the hell?

I grab his arm, trying to yank myself free without revealing too much of who I am to these men.

"Do you see how her cheeks flushed a bright crimson pink when I said she was a virgin? Do you see how she dresses? How she reacts to your stares through her almost sheer dress? Have any of you seen her before, even though she lives amongst us?"

Silence.

"I've had her watched for ages, knowing she would one day ask for this arrangement. I've never seen her with a man. I could call for a doctor to examine her, but that would do little more than prolong this process. Once we sell her first kiss, it will be obvious to you all. And if it's not, then you'll get to experience her for free if it can be proven that she's not a virgin."

Peter releases me as murmurs spread through the room. My eyes lock on one man—the man who has proof that I'm a liar. That I did share one first with a man—a kiss.

It was more than a kiss. It was kisses. It was touches. It was grinding and indecency, and I shouldn't have stopped him. I should have let Hayes take everything. I could have still sold my body, my life to a man here, but I would have experienced everything first. It's true I wouldn't have gotten the same level of money, but surely I would have gotten six figures in total—enough for my family to survive on for a while.

Hayes, with his green eyes and soft smile, stares at me, meeting my gaze with a knowing look of his own.

Damn him, he's going to rat me out. Even if I am a virgin in all other ways, it's not going to matter. The others won't believe it, and I'm going to lose lots of money if Hayes outs me.

But then the man gives the tiniest shake of his head—letting me know our secret is safe.

I let out a breath and quickly tear my gaze from the only man here I would want to have kiss me, touch me, fuck me. That is until I realized he's the kind of man to frequent these events. Now I want to destroy him like I want to destroy every man here.

"Good, then we will start with the first round of bidding —her first kiss," Peter says.

Here we go.

I lick my lips automatically, as if trying to entice these suckers to bid more on me. I can't imagine anyone spending much money to be the first to kiss me. I'm not expecting much—a couple of thousand dollars if I'm lucky.

"The winning bid will have twenty minutes to claim as many first kisses as he wants from her. But he can only kiss where her skin is currently exposed, nothing beneath her clothes."

My skin crawls—twenty minutes to kiss one of these vile men. *How am I not going to puke midway through?*

"Let's start the bidding at fifty thousand," Peter says.

My jaw drops. No man here is going to pay fifty grand to kiss me for twenty minutes.

But hands immediately fly in the air. My heart stutters in fear at what I'm doing here. I thought I was strong enough, determined enough, cold enough. I thought I would easily be able to shield myself from what the expectations of me would be when they only paid a couple thousand for a kiss. I can't imagine what's going to be expected of me for fifty thousand.

Peter starts chattering like a true auctioneer, and I can barely keep up with the bidding. My eyes fly around the room at each man as they lift their hand, bidding on me. I don't know who I want to win. I don't know any of the men here. Most aren't attractive. Most are at least a decade or two older than me. But there are a handful of men who are close in age to me and are mildly attractive. I would prefer any of them.

And then my eyes flicker to Hayes. I meant to let my eyes just pass over him like I have every other man here, but when I look at him, I know who I want to win. I want him to win every round.

But if what Peter says is true, Hayes is nothing but a playboy with little money. He won't try to win me in the end. The best I'll get is for him to win one of these early rounds.

More bidding happens, though, and yet Hayes doesn't raise his hand—not once.

He already got to kiss me for free—*why pay for another kiss?*

"Going once...going twice..." Peter starts. "First kiss sold for one hundred and fifty thousand dollars."

My head snaps back to Peter. *Who bought my first kiss?* I missed it because I was pining for Hayes, wishing my life was different.

No, I don't want a different life. I don't want the life of any other Retribution King. This is my destiny—this life. I know I can make a change, one that will ripple through every Retribution King in existence. I just have to endure.

"I have the largest bedroom already set up. Anyone interested must pay ten thousand to watch. We will start in thirty minutes, after the funds have been received," Peter says like he's announcing dinner time.

A man with a gleam in his bright blue eyes approaches Peter beside me. "I doubt she's going to go through with this. Look at her. She's trembling. Why did you bring us here just to watch her change her mind? We aren't rapists. We won't force her. You knew better than to arrange this, Peter."

Suddenly, my body stops trembling. My hands clench at my side, and a strong drumming energy builds inside my chest like a hurricane force about to explode on this man.

He's wrong—so very wrong.

I stare him down. The man's vicious scowl drops from his face as his eyes widen at the sight of me. I decide to make sure there aren't any other doubters in the room.

"To whoever bought me, feel free to pay an additional hundred thousand, and you can tie me up if you want. That goes for any round—wouldn't want me to run away. And as I'm consenting now, it's not rape. I very much want this."

The man's stunned expression spreads across his face. Chuckles and murmurs bounce through the room like wildfire.

The moment is intense. I take a deep breath *in...and out...*I close my eyes as I continue breathing, and I remember *why* I'm here. *What* I must do to make things right. And *who* I am.

When I snap my eyes open, it's with a new determination. I'm not going to fear this—any of it. There is nothing to fear. Tonight it will be a kiss, later a touch, an orgasm, a fuck. All of it will be because I want it. All of it will be because these suckers are willing to pay thousands of dollars for the joy of thinking they are stealing something from me that I couldn't care less about.

Love isn't real. It's not something I've ever wanted. It's a weakness. It's not something I've ever searched for.

This is all just a business arrangement—one where I get the better end of the deal. One hundred and fifty thousand dollars, more if he wants to tie me up, more if others decide to watch. That's more money than my family has seen in the last decade. That money alone will keep them fed and possibly even stretch to their current rent for many years to come.

And it's all for a kiss. *What will they pay for more than a kiss?*

I start to walk forward, deciding I should spend the rest of my time mingling to see if I can get these men to fall further under my spell so they'll pay more for me next round, but Peter grabs my forearm.

"You should wait in the bedroom. You're mysterious to them. You don't want them to know you. The longer they have to wait to find out, the more enticing you will be to them. And when they finally get a bite, they'll keep coming back for more," he says.

I consider Peter's words, but it doesn't feel like a choice. If I don't go to the bedroom, he'll drag me there kicking and screaming.

I won't show weakness. I won't let them see any fear. Because it would be a lie if they did. I'm not afraid of anything. Not anymore. Not after the life I've lived.

I nod, and Peter leads me to a bedroom that was locked when I first arrived. He unlocks the door and leads me inside.

"We'll start shortly. Make yourself comfortable."

Peter leaves, and I stare around the room with shaky legs.

I'm not afraid.

I'm not scared.

I have no fear.

I repeat the words to myself as I see a chair with leather restraints draped over one of the armrests in the center of the room. The lighting is such that the edges of the room are cast in dark shadows with only a spotlight in the center.

I gulp lungfuls of air, which appears to be in thin supply in this room. And then I still, returning to the strength I had when I faced down the man who taunted me before.

I am not afraid. There is nothing to fear. They should fear me.

CHAPTER 9

Hayes

I STEP INTO THE BEDROOM, already knowing what to expect. I've been to these events several times, always to gather information and to get the other men there to trust me. But this time is different. This time, more than any others, I want to grab the woman being auctioned off, kidnap her, and save her from this life.

But if I were to do that, I'd be signing a death sentence for both of us. The Retribution Kings would never stop until they saw us dead. And even if I were to save Lilith, I'm not sure it's what she would want. She chose this. She wants this auction to happen. To save her family, yes, but there appears to be more to her motivation. I haven't figured out all the pieces yet, but I will. And when I do, I'll find a way to help her.

Yes, I have my own mission, but somehow in a single moment, Lilith became more important to me. The sooner I can help her, the sooner I can give my full attention back to my own mission.

I stare at the floor, unable to look at her—not yet. I've

paid to be able to watch, but watching her being kissed by another man will be torture. I don't know how I'm going to survive any of the other rounds. My enemies couldn't find a better way to torture me if they tried.

But I can't wait outside the room either. I have to watch over her. If she gives the slightest signal that she wants this to stop—I'll end it, even if it ruins both our lives.

Every man who showed up tonight paid the extra money to watch her get kissed. We're standing shoulder to shoulder in the shadows, lining the wall. As I continue to stare at the floor, Peter speaks.

"Mr. Collier, the room is yours for the next twenty minutes. And as you agreed to pay the extra hundred thousand to tie her up, the restraints are next to the chair."

Fuck.

I know why Lilith said what she said, but I'm not sure her being tied up is going to make this easier for her. At least Daniel Collier isn't a cruel man. He isn't too old. And he's a good enough-looking man. Kissing him shouldn't be too much of a hardship.

My anxiety gets the better of me, and I can't look away any longer. I see Lilith standing under the spotlight, looking toward Daniel as he steps out from the shadows. The corner of her mouth lifts up, seemingly pleased by the man who won the first auction.

I don't know why he paid to tie her up; I've never seen him tie up any other woman at an event like this before. Daniel always seems like a genuinely nice man. He always bids early and high, ensuring the woman ends up with good money no matter what. And he always seems interested in learning if he and the woman would make a good match. Once he determines they won't be, he never bids again. He rarely even watches the later rounds. I'm guessing he thought he'd get crap from the other guys if he didn't agree to tie her up.

Daniel steps further into the light, and Lilith doesn't move. She doesn't flinch or tremble or show any fear. Quite the opposite—her face lights up as if she's the one in control here.

I bite my lip, holding back my own grin. It usually takes the women a couple of rounds to realize how much power they hold. Lilith realized it immediately. She's different than the rest. She needs money, sure. She probably even needs a high-ranking Retribution King husband. This is a way for her to get both, but there is something else about her. It's the same thing that draws me to her. I see myself in her. Even if she's the grumpiness to my sunshine, we're more alike than different.

Lilith licks her lips slowly and intentionally. She stands straighter, pushing her breasts against the thin fabric of her dress until her nipples are puckering against soft cotton. With the way the light is shining down on her, I can make out the silhouette of her body.

Fuck, why didn't I bid? What fucking torture is this? I finally found a woman I want. She's perfect for me—I knew within five minutes of meeting her. And yet, I can't have her. She will never, ever be mine.

It's the cruelest thing I've ever endured.

Maybe she could be mine, the devil whispers over my shoulder.

Daniel steps into the light, his eyes dilating with lust at seeing her trying to seduce him. He reaches his hand out and strokes down her cheek, before gripping the ends of her red ringlets.

Lilith's eyes lock on Daniel's, and for a moment, I think she truly wants him. He's exactly her type. Even if he wasn't paying for the opportunity, she'd willingly kiss him, go on a date with him, maybe even marry him. That is until I remember how she looked when I kissed her. How the crave desire swirled around her eyes. How she tried to hide her attraction, but it was impossible to contain.

This is an act. *To make her appear strong? Or to make herself feel like she wants this?* It doesn't matter.

Daniel can't do much touching without Peter stopping him, but he does run his hands down her sides to her hips. He then walks her backward until the back of her thighs hit the chair and pushes her down to sit.

They don't speak to each other. She doesn't taunt him. And he doesn't boss her around.

Wordlessly, he takes the leather restraints in his hand and kneels between her legs. Lilith's response is to rake her teeth over her bottom lip, teasing him into thinking she wants him more than any man here when I know that isn't true. This is a job to her—a way to make a lot of money quickly.

She wants me.

I don't think that because I'm cocky and think I'm better than any man here. I say it because I know it's true, truer than anything I've ever believed before.

Daniel wraps the leather restraint around her left ankle, tightening it until her leg is flush against the leg of the chair. Then he moves to her other leg, hiking her dress up enough so he gets access to her calf before dropping the dress back down.

He moves slowly and methodically while his gaze never leaves her starry-eyed one. His hands move to her wrists, binding them just as securely to the chair. Then she's bound to the chair, completely at his whim.

He's wasted much of his time tying her up and not kissing her, but I understand the arousal that happens before the kiss. The air in the room is thick with lust and desire. Every man here wants her and wishes they were Daniel.

Finally, his lips come down on top of hers.

It's a silent kiss. His eyes close. Hers remain open.

My foot starts to move toward her before my brain kicks in. I force myself to stop.

This is her choice. She wants this. She had other choices.

My stomach turns as Daniel parts her lips with his tongue. I remember how it felt when I did the same thing. How hot and inviting her mouth was. How she felt like home but also my greatest adventure, all tied together in one kiss. I have to find a way to stop this. I can't endure this every night, and she deserves better.

Suddenly, Daniel draws back—just a millimeter away from her lips. He doesn't make a sound, but I can see the way her eyes dilate in a wicked gleam. His tongue quickly sweeps over his bottom lip, catching a tiny drop of blood.

I grin.

Good, he deserves to know who's in control. It's her, not us.

Daniel presses his lips against hers harder, forcing more of his lips and tongue into her than before. He's trying to pretend that he owns her, but she's too great for any of us.

I hold my breath. *Don't let this break you, Lilith. Please. I'll find a way to help you, I promise.*

When I open my eyes, I see her green eyes cut in my direction. She can't see me in the shadows, but for a moment, I think she can. And I think she's trying to send me a message.

I cock my head to the side, confused as to what she's trying to say, before her eyes go back to watching Daniel kiss her.

I scan her head to toe, trying to make sense of what she was saying. *What am I missing?*

And then I see it.

I grin, biting back a chuckle as I see where her arm has broken free of the bindings. It's not obvious. And I'm not sure if she's going to do anything or not, but it's the fact that she did break free easily. Lilith's much more than she seems. And I vow to learn every one of her darkest secrets.

CHAPTER 10

Lilith

SOMETHING DEPRAVED AWAKENS in me when Daniel's lips press against mine. I know why I'm here, why I agreed to this contract. Why I agreed to this absurd bet where I supposedly lose more and more of myself, where I let them take every piece of me bit by bit.

None of them realize how false that is. Despite this game where they bet and take and take and take, they won't be taking anything from me. I'll be the one doing all the taking. I knew what I was doing from the moment my pen signed my name, and yet, this darkness swirling deep in the cavity of my chest, encircling my heart, twisting it into a dark and wicked beast was not in the plans. I never meant to awaken the sleeping animal within me. My monster was buried so deep within me after what happened, I didn't think it would ever return again.

One kiss did that.

One stupid, not even good, kiss.

I've had very little practice with kisses up until this point, but Daniel kisses like a puppy dog. Wet and slimy and with too much tongue, there is nothing to be enjoyed.

Hayes—my mind immediately goes to his kiss. There was nothing wrong with the way that man kissed. Then again, he's a playboy, so kissing skills are to be expected. But he didn't have to kiss me as if trying to make me orgasm with just his tongue on my lips. I shake the thought from my head. I can't allow myself to get turned on by thoughts of Hayes while kissing Daniel.

But in not thinking about Hayes, I grow bored. The ominous darkness swirls in intensity in my chest, brewing like a poisonous elixir I'm about to unleash on the world.

I wasn't sure how far I'd go before this moment. Now I know—nothing is far enough. No pain goes too far. No retribution is enough.

"Time is up," Peter says.

Daniel backs away immediately with a smug expression across his pretty boy face. I bat my eyelashes at him and wink, pretending he just gave me the best damn kiss of my life.

He reaches out, letting his thumb brush against my bottom lip. His cheeky grin begs me to engrain the memory of that kiss in my brain.

Don't worry, I won't be forgetting that kiss anytime soon. Or you, Daniel Collier.

My dark gaze bares into his back as he walks out of the room.

I don't move a muscle as I listen to the other men slowly file out of the room. Only once the door closes on a silent and empty room do I move my hands free of the bindings. Then I bend down and undo the ropes on my ankles.

The door creaks open again, as I sit in the chair unbound. Peter stares at me, unfazed by me getting out of the bindings.

"You have one hour," he says before leaving the room again.

One hour—not nearly enough. And yet, far too long.

I run out of the room. Two steps out, and I hear the men from the living room discussing playing poker while they wait.

These fuckers have too much money to just keep it in their pockets all day. They have to spend every waken moment trying to spend their money. They couldn't possibly think of a way to use that money to help others.

I need air.

I noticed a balcony off one of the guest bedrooms in my earlier tour of the room, and I beeline for it. Keeping my head down, I don't look at the others, and I don't ask permission from Peter or tell him where I'm going. I'll be back when my precious hour is up.

Vengeance sweeps through me like a bat through a cave. This is why I was born. This is my purpose.

The cool air hits my face as I burst through the sliding glass door and out onto the small balcony. Most of the space is taken by two small chairs and an end table. I run straight for the railing and hold on as I take a deep breath, my entire body rejoicing at the air going through my nostrils and deep into my lungs.

"You're not going to jump, are you? I couldn't live with that on my conscience," Hayes says from behind me, his playful, charming voice unmistakable.

My heart snaps back into place, my shields go up, and the monster stirring tries to decide which battle I'll choose.

"It wouldn't be your fault if I did."

"Wouldn't it be? I'm here, betting on you. I'm a willing participant driving you to want to end it all rather than endure a bunch of horny, vile men, thinking they can pay money to have the honor of doing whatever they want with your body."

"You didn't bet on me." I raise an eyebrow and turn my head to face him.

"No, I didn't."

"You got to kiss me for free. Are you going to out me? Let Daniel know that he overpaid since it wasn't my first kiss?"

He takes a step toward me. His eyes glisten behind his full-framed glasses, a secret in them he's teasing me with. His gaze matches his overzealous grin. *Why the hell is the man always smiling?* He can't have something to be that happy about all the time.

An ache builds between my thighs, and my nipples harden under his greedy gaze. He doesn't shy away from looking at my body. He doesn't hide the fact that he's staring through my too-thin fabric, memorizing every curve of my body. And I don't hide my annoyance that his staring is doing things to my body that I can't control.

"Stop that," I say.

He cocks his head, his grin curling higher as he chuckles deeply. Then he takes another step closer, invading my space but not touching me. The fresh air that I came out here to breathe becomes dense. Suddenly, I'm hit with an undeniable urge to rip out his hair tie and run my hand through his brown locks as I kiss him, knocking his stupid grin off his face.

"Stop what, exactly?"

I shake my head. "What do you want? Why did you follow me?"

His smile instantly drops, and a shadow falls over his face. His features dull, hiding the bright, flirting persona he uses as a cover to hide something dark within him. Or maybe that's just me projecting on him, and he really is this happy, joyful person all the time.

No one is this happy all the time. He's hiding something.

"To save you."

His words snap me out of my head. "Save me?"

He nods, his eyes studying me carefully as he puts his hands in his pockets.

"Save me? You think I need saving?"

He nods again. *It's annoying.*

"I don't need saving." I narrow my eyes, and my lips curl into a snarl.

"Ten million."

"What?" His words stop me in my tracks from wanting to rip out his throat.

"Ten million dollars to end this. Your family can live comfortably for the rest of their lives, and you'll have enough money to pursue your own dreams. Ten million to save you, right now."

My jaw falls open for a second. My heart thumps rapidly at his offer before I realize the truth. "You don't have ten million dollars. You don't have a million dollars. I doubt you have much more money than I do."

"It doesn't matter if I do or don't. What matters is whether or not you'll accept my offer? If you do, I'll have the money."

"You'll do what? Steal for it?" I fold my arms over my chest and stare at him with contempt.

"I'll do whatever it takes." His eyes smolder with possession—he'd do anything to make me his.

I gulp, my body hot with an uncontrollable desire flushing through me. But I push the urge down, locking it up where the monster inside me used to sleep.

"And the contract I signed?"

"Don't worry about the contract. I'd have it destroyed."

I shake my head. "I know your past, Hayes. Your loyalty has been questioned already, and I doubt destroying my contract would help your case. We'd be running from the

Retribution Kings for the rest of our lives, until they killed us."

"I'm friends with the new King of the Retribution Kings—Titus. I would have your contract amended. We wouldn't run. We'd have no need. It wouldn't be a death sentence, very much the opposite."

"I don't need saving."

His expression doesn't change. He doesn't seem shocked at all.

It was a test. This is a test. He was never going to give me ten million dollars to stop this. He didn't care to save me. He wanted to know if I was doing this for the money or for some other reason. I don't know how he guessed it. I don't know how he knows the truth, but he does. Which means I'm at risk of others finding out before I can fulfill my duty.

"Who do you work for?"

"Myself," I snap back.

His jaw clenches as he looks over me. "You don't have to worry about others finding out. None of them are as observant as I am."

"You're not observant, just horny. You think you can throw money at me and sweep me off my feet? You think you're my Prince Charming saving me, when you're only offering me a trade of prisons? Instead of getting far more money from the highest bidder, I'd end up chained to you for only ten million."

"Yes, but you like me. And I can fulfill all those dirty desires spinning around in your head. None of those men can. None of them know what to do with you, how to make you come, how to keep you satisfied."

I shake my head. "So cocky and full of yourself."

"I am because I speak from experience. I'm good at two things, Lilith—cooking and making women come."

I narrow my eyes at his words—*making women come. Not fucking women, interesting.*

And still, his words stir something in my core, something I'm begging for a man to bring to life. *He's a fucking good kisser. How would it feel for his tongue to be on my clit? For his cock to be buried inside me?*

Stop, it will never happen.

Hayes steps forward until his chest is brushing against mine.

My feet try to step back, and my hands reach back, gripping the railing behind me. I'm trapped, and yet, Hayes doesn't do anything. He doesn't really touch me. He would let me go if I said the words.

Instead, my breathing is ragged and uneven.

"Tell me the truth, Lilith. Tell me your plan."

"Why?" I shudder, loving the way he says my name like he's already in love with me. But he can't be. He's just a charmer. Even though I know it's an act, he still makes my fucking heart beat like he's the most fascinating man on the face of the earth.

Traitorous heart.

"I believe you and I might be on the same side, Lilith Hart."

As my name again falls from his thick lips in his deep voice, it's easy to imagine my name escaping his mouth as he comes.

I grind my teeth together so harshly I might crack a molar, and my fists clench. I need anything to distract me from this feeling between us.

"You're a male Retribution King, an outcast one slowly regaining his place. You are very much on the opposing side. We're not the same, you and me."

He frowns. It feels wrong to see him frown, and I realize now why he never does it.

"I think we are, but only time will tell." He takes a step back, and I can breathe deeply for the first time since he stepped out here.

"I can't promise you anything. I wish you'd taken my deal—you shouldn't have to suffer alone. But in the end, you'll end up as mine."

And then Hayes disappears back inside. He thinks he knows me, but he doesn't understand me at all.

CHAPTER 11

Hayes

I SHOULD HAVE STAYED out on the balcony with Lilith. Gage is standing in the hallway when I step back inside.

This can't be good.

No, I should have thrown her stubborn ass over my shoulder and forced her to go with me. This is madness. She doesn't have to endure any of it because I can protect her.

And yet she refused me.

Gage is lurking quietly in the dark shadows of the hallway—his dark skin making it even harder to see him. But his intense stare always gets my skin crawling.

"I'm guessing you aren't here to bid on my girl?" I ask, with a peppiness in my voice I don't feel. But that's who I am—the jokester, the fun one. Gage gets to be serious, while I have to laugh and lighten the mood. It's who we both are, and I can't change anymore than he can.

He stares at me, and I sigh.

"What's up?" I ask.

He glances past me, into the full penthouse living room. "What the hell are you doing?"

I've known Gage for a long time. He wants what's best for me as much as I want what's best for him, but I won't let him deter me.

"My job," I answer, yawning.

"Don't pull that crap with me, Hayes. You're risking everything."

"I'm really not."

"Do you even know who she is?"

"She's Lilith Hart. She's brave and grumpy and loyal to her family." *And she has her own agenda I'm still trying to figure out, but I'm not going to tell him that, or he's really not going to like what I'm doing.*

He shakes his head, running his hand over his shaved head. "I don't like it. Do your job, yes, but don't sleep with her. Don't fall for her."

I scoff. "Am I known for falling in love? I don't think I've ever been in love."

His dark eyes skim over mine as if searching for a clue. When Gage goes searching, he always finds something.

"I think we should talk to Lennox, see what he thinks about your choices."

I roll my eyes. "Going to tell daddy on me, really?"

"This is a decision we should all make together."

"No, it's not. Lennox completed his task, his way. I'm going to do the same."

"You can't fall in love."

"Lennox did, but you don't have to worry about me. I won't fall in love." I'm pretty sure I already have, but admitting that to him would be a bad move on my part. He'd think I'm insane. I don't know her. I've barely spent any time with her. I can't be in love. And yet, I know I am.

And I already know I'm putting everything at risk by loving her. I don't even know what my next move is. I know how to complete my mission, but I don't know how to end up with her. I don't know how to save her. I'm not even sure if I care if I get her in the end as long as she's happy. I want Lilith to be happy and stop this foolish game.

"What are you doing here other than lecturing me? Are you going to bid on Lilith?" If he does, I'm probably going to kill him. As it is, I already have a kill list. I may be trying to get back on the Retribution King's good side, but any man who touches Lilith deserves to die.

"Just reminding you of your job. Don't fuck this up, Hayes."

"Why does everyone think I'm going to fuck things up? Lennox fucked up a lot of shit. Things are already very complicated, so I can't make anything worse." *I'm totally going to make it worse. Fuck.*

Gage gives me one of his long stares, the serious kind supposed to inspire fear to make me behave.

"Five-minute warning," I hear Peter from the room behind me.

"That's my cue." I grin and turn away from Gage.

I sigh when he can no longer see me.

I can't fuck this up. Gage is right. I have to put some distance between me and Lilith. She can't be mine for so many reasons. Maybe someday, but not someday soon.

I just need to make sure she's better off without me. Right now, I'm her best option, as far as I can tell.

Lilith returns to the living room a few minutes after me, looking more radiant than I've ever seen her. She's redone her makeup and tamed some of her curls. I can't decide if I prefer the tamed or wild look better.

Most notably, she's calm. She's almost unfazed by the beginning of another auction.

Her eyes cut to me, and she winks. It's all a game to her. I just wish I knew what game she was playing and how to help her win.

Is she really a virgin?

Does she like to fuck for money?

Or does she think this is her only choice?

I saw what she did before, getting free of the restraints. *But what does that mean? Is she really strong enough to fight back? Or is just knowing that she is in control and could stop it at any moment enough for her? Is she just a fortune hunter, looking for the wealthiest man here to marry her? Is she power-hungry?*

I have so many questions about who Lilith is, but all I know for sure is that she's forbidden. I can't have her, and it makes me want her even more.

She flips her hair side to side, and I have to bite my lip to keep from growling possessively. *She's fucking mine.*

I grin at her, pretending I'm fine with what she's doing. She can fuck the whole damn room, and I'll keep smiling. I'm fine. She's not ripping my heart and soul out.

Is she faking or not? The way she stares down every man here makes me think she wants this, but maybe she wants me to think that.

Peter starts the bidding, but I'm barely paying attention. I'm not sure what the bids are for, what pieces of her the winning bidder gets to claim.

I study her. I watch her more intensely than I ever have before, trying to put together the pieces of the puzzle. But I can't quite figure her out.

"Harvey wins," Peter says.

I blink.

And Lilith's head snaps to me.

I didn't bid.

Again.

And it affected her.

Did she want me to bid? Is this one of the moments where

she says she doesn't want me to save her, but I'm supposed to anyway?

"I'm not going to pay to watch Harvey strip her naked. I'd rather play another round of poker," Reuben mutters beside me. Some of the men chuckle in agreement.

A few pay Peter to watch.

"Hayes? You paying or playing?" Reuben asks.

I feel Lilith's stare on me and hear Gage's words in my head.

"Deal me in," I say, sitting down at one of the poker tables. I notice Lilith out of the corner of my eye, and I swear her lips fall in disappointment. Maybe that's my imagination, or maybe it's just Lilith. She doesn't smile often, preferring to grimace and glare at everyone.

Whether Lilith wants me to save her or not, she'll be mostly safe this round. Removing her clothing is nothing, even though I'm dying to see her naked. I need to prove to myself and to Gage that I have restraint.

I still put our brotherhood above everything else. What Lennox, Gage, and I have been through is the thing I care most about. It's not love; it's just lust. It's just my dick talking and the horny situation of this auction.

But I can't keep my eyes off the bedroom door as I play poker with a few of the guys. I can't keep thinking I made a huge mistake. I should have thrown her over my shoulder and ran. Or I should have told Titus I couldn't be his second any longer and let her survive her own fate.

That's what I should do—tell Titus I resign and to find someone else to do his dirty work. I don't need the Retribution King leader on my side to complete my mission, even if it would help me.

A loud bang comes from the bedroom, drawing everyone's attention. The game stops, and our heads snap to the door.

What the hell?

Screams rip through the air, and fear seers through my body as more gunfire erupts inside the room.

I jump up and run, knocking my chair back. I'm the first one to the door, but it's locked.

Motherfucker. I pull my gun out and fire at the handle, before kicking the door in.

The room is dark. There are no lights. Men are scurrying around, weapons drawn, but I can't see an immediate threat.

"Lilith?" I yell through the darkness. My eyes scan, and I move toward the center of the room, where I'm guessing she's tied up.

My legs hit the side of a bed, and my hands come down on a bedsheet, feeling for her body. Eventually, warm flesh hits my fingertips. Warm, not cold—she's not dead.

"Lilith!" I grab onto her and begin to pull her into my arms before realizing she's tied to the bed when her body barely budges.

"Undo your arms," I command her, while I tend to her ankles.

I don't know if she's listening to me or not, but a second later, when I yank her body up, she's completely free. I run out of the room with Lilith's naked body in my arms. I don't know where I'm going, but I don't stop. I'm not sure I ever will.

CHAPTER 12

Lilith

HAYES CRADLES me in his arms as he runs—and runs and runs. My body should be bouncing up and down from how fast he's moving, but he's holding me so close and tightly that I feel like I'm being gently rocked to sleep.

I can't make sense of what's happening or even how I ended up in his arms exactly. The world is going by in a whirl of lights and darkness. All I know is he's taking me away. It's probably for the best. I shouldn't stay here; I'll end up dead if I do.

I close my eyes as my head snuggles into his suit jacket. A minute later, they open to the pop of a hotel room door. Hayes carries me inside before closing the door gently behind him.

"Sorry I woke you," he says as he stares down at me still in his arms.

I frown. He's apologizing to me. He's such a strange man, and I can't make sense of him. All I know is that I don't trust him.

"You can put me down now."

His eyes drop playfully to my body, something mischievous in his bright green eyes.

I follow his gaze and realize I'm naked. Blood streaks across my stomach and breasts, coating my hands.

"How about a bath?" he asks.

I nod, not sure what else to say.

With a sweet smile, he carries me into the bathroom. He flicks on the tub with his foot, never putting me down. His eyes meet mine, keeping his gaze from rolling over my naked body.

Hmm.

The water fills, and we both just stare at each other in silence. I wait for him to ask what happened or to explain why he took me or what we're doing here, but he doesn't.

Instead, he starts humming brightly. He's so nonchalant; it's like he's waiting on his coffee, not waiting for a tub to fill so he can clean the blood off me. I would ask why he has any interest in me at all, except it's clear that after we kissed, he thinks he owns some part of me like every man here does. Maybe he's even looking for another freebie, just trying to avoid paying for me.

Yes, that must be it.

The tub fills, and he once again turns it off with his foot.

"I'm going to lower you into the tub. I want to stay, since I don't think you should be alone right now, but I'll leave if you'd prefer some privacy."

I narrow my eyes in confusion as I stare up into his. "Privacy," I say.

He nods, his jaw tensing and his smile vanishing.

I watch his face carefully as he lowers me gently into the tub. He doesn't look at my naked body as he does it. The warmth of the tub caresses my aching body and soothes my soul. But even with the warm water, I start trembling at the sight of my bloody hands the second I leave Hayes's arms.

Soon, my entire body is trembling so much that the water is splashing against the sides of the tub.

Hayes reaches in and takes my hand in his. He grabs a washcloth and begins scrubbing the blood from my right hand, washing it away so quickly I'm not sure it was ever there. Quickly, he does the same to my left.

I stare at my hands, shaking a little less but still shaking.

Hayes takes my right hand again and begins rubbing my palm in slow circles with the pad of his thumb. Then he just waits with me, waits for the stillness to return.

I close my eyes to avoid staring at the red-hued water and let my head fall back against the edge of the tub. Hayes doesn't leave like I initially requested, but he does give me privacy with my thoughts. I don't feel his bright stare on me; I just feel his hand on mine. It sends warm tingles through my body that, for once, I welcome.

And then I'm back in that room.

Harvey's jet-black eyes staring at me with a hunger and cruelty I've never seen before in a man. His snicker as he stares at me tied to the bed. The shine of the knife he pulls from his pocket. The applause and cheers as he shows what he plans to use to undress me.

My stomach knotting, and my breathing shaky as he used that knife to slice through my dress like it was paper. Him letting the blade slip too close to my skin and laughing as he nicked my soft belly.

I wince like it's happening again.

It won't ever happen again.

My eyes fly open, and I'm back in the bathroom. Hayes is still holding my hand.

"Why did you take me?" I shout at Hayes.

He grins. *He fucking grins at me.*

"What?" I ask.

"You, Lilith. You're incredible. I save you from possibly

being murdered, and you act like I was the one who ripped your clothes off and threatened your life."

"You might as well have. You're just like them! You're a Retribution King. You came to the event. And for whatever reason, you thought playing poker was more interesting than watching me get stripped by an old man with a gut and sick fantasy. Was it so you could keep your conscious clean? Pretend what was happening to me wasn't? Or because getting my clothes cut off by an old man isn't enough excitement to pay ten grand for?"

He's staring at me with love in his eyes. His gaze says I'm his acting like his perfect woman, not like I just gave him a tongue lashing.

In the excitement, I unknowingly raised out of the tub enough to expose my breasts. I quickly cover my hands over them, but not before Hayes gets a look.

I blush red. "Get out!"

He lets go of my hand and bites his lip but doesn't move.

"Are you deaf? Get out!"

He chuckles softly as my blush deepens. The softness of his voice tugs at my heart just a little. It's not enough to change my mind, though.

And then his smile drops like a door being slammed shut. "You're injured."

"I...uh...yea," I exhale. "Harvey cut me."

His eyes turn murderous as a dark wave of emotion I would have never guessed could cross his face takes hold. He stares deeply at the string of cuts that disappear down the center of my stomach under the water.

Then he studies my face, and a goofy grin spreads across his cheeks as an idea forms in his head.

He stands, quickly pulling his jacket off and his shirt over his head.

"What are you doing?" My eyes widen, and my mouth

waters as I stare at his naked chest. He's muscled and ripped with that delicious V at his hips. I want to run my tongue over it and...

Jesus, what am I thinking? He's just a good kisser. That's it!

And then he's undoing his pants.

"Hayes...Hayes, stop; what are you doing?"

"Making you smile," he grins. He lowers his pants in one swift motion, now completely naked in front of me.

My jaw falls open, and my eyes pop as I stare at him. I can't avert my eyes, can't look anywhere else but him. The V of his lean hips leads my gaze to his thickening cock.

"Oh my god! It's...it's..."

"It seems I leave you speechless quite a lot. And yes, my dick is pierced."

"Jesus, did that hurt?"

He shrugs.

I study him closer, trying to see past the facade he puts up. But he hides his truth well.

He wiggles his eyebrows at me, and I smile softly.

His shoulders relax at that sight. "Your smile is beautiful. It makes it even more special when you make me work for it."

I chuckle. "I'm not sure how you stripping naked was supposed to make me smile, but I'm not going to tell you to dress."

"Good, now let me tend to your wounds while your eyes take in every inch of me."

I shake my head, not able to get off the smile across my lips just yet. "It won't take that long to take in every inch of you. You aren't that big."

"Ouch," he chuckles as he presses a washcloth over the cut on my stomach. He reaches into the tub to drain the water as his eyes look over the shallow cuts.

He grabs a towel and drapes it over my shoulders, before lifting me up gently, his arms underneath my shoulders and legs. He carries me swiftly into the bedroom and lays me down on the bed.

"Wait here."

I lift an eyebrow. "Not sure where I'd go naked except for a towel."

He chuckles low and deep.

He goes back into the bathroom, and a few minutes later, he returns with some bandaids and pain reliever.

He hands me the pills, and I take them dry. While he quickly covers my cuts in thin bandaids, a deep scowl so uncharacteristic of him blanches his face whenever he looks at the cuts. When he's finished, he wraps the towel around me, covering my body.

His eyes lift to mine, and that glorious grin of his reappears. Somehow, this smile has a wicked flare to it.

"Now are you going to tell me what you're up to?" he says.

I pull the towel tight around my chest with one hand. "What do you mean? I'm not up to anything other than getting as much money for my family as possible."

"You were the cause of the bloodshed in that room. And if I know you as well as I think I know you, then you aimed to kill. My guess is Harvey is dead. Possibly even Daniel if you got the chance."

I suck in a breath. *Fuck, he knows.*

I was careful.

I hid my actions so there would be no way for the others in that room to know if it was me or someone else who killed their friends. I retied myself to the bed after. I screamed in fear. And I only attacked when the lights went low, stabbing Harvey from behind with his own knife so there was no way anyone would guess it was me.

How did Hayes figure it out? He wasn't even in the room! And once the others know, what punishment will I receive?

My instincts kick in, and I do the only thing I can think to do. This is Hayes's hotel room. I reach under the pillow I'm leaning against, hoping to find some weapon—a gun or knife—something to escape.

My hand finds a knife.

I keep my expression blank as I press it in the palm of my hand, and my fingers curl around the hilt.

Hayes leans into me, that grin still there. His green eyes bare into mine, begging me to trust him.

I don't. And he shouldn't trust me, either.

"It's okay. I can help you," he says.

It's a lie.

He wants to know the truth so he can figure out how to use it against me. He's just like the rest of them, trying to figure out what retribution he should seek.

His smile falters a second, sensing what I'm about to do, but he doesn't stop me. I swing the knife into his chest and run.

CHAPTER 13

Hayes

LILITH STABBED ME. *She fucking stabbed me.*

My lips curl up. I'm falling in love with her even more.

I stumble up, the pain in my chest throbbing. I want to lie down on the bed until the pain subsides, but it's not going to anytime soon. I stagger into the bathroom, gripping the sink as I take a look at the damage.

My knife is jabbed into my chest, with blood oozing around the impact. It's high in my chest—completely missing my lungs or heart. It pierced the skin just below the clavicle, missing the muscles of my shoulder and any major arteries.

I'm still grinning like the fool I am. Lilith just stabbed me. I should be angry. I should be planning my retribution. Instead, my heart is doing somersaults in my chest when I think about her.

My phone vibrates in my pants pocket on the floor. I kneel down gingerly to pick it up, seeing Gage's name flash across the screen.

"What's up?" I answer, doing my best to keep my voice light and the pain out of my voice.

"Harvey, Daniel, and Jonathan are dead."

Holy shit!

I don't respond as I stare at the knife sticking out of my chest. She killed them, yet I was an easier target. I should be dead right now. Instead, she only aimed to injure me.

My grin grows wider, and my eyes light up at that. It's not a confession of her love for me, but at least she doesn't want me dead like Harvey and Daniel. And Jonathan? He never did anything to her. I'm not even sure she knew who he was.

"Hayes, are you listening to me? What the hell happened? Are we—"

"How were they killed?" I interrupt.

"Harvey and Daniel were stabbed. Jonathan was shot in the back of the head. My best guess is at least two attackers."

My gut says she didn't kill Jonathan. *How would she have gotten her hands on both a knife and a gun? Even if she didn't do it herself, is she working with someone else? Or was it friendly fire trying to take out the attacker?*

"Are there more attackers coming? Who killed them?" Gage asks with a panic in his voice.

"No, we're not under attack. We have nothing to worry about. If anything, this is a good distraction while everyone tries to figure out who killed them. I can complete my mission without anyone noticing me."

"You know who killed them?"

"Yes," I confirm.

"And?"

"And it doesn't matter. They aren't a threat to us."

"How do you know that? You can't complete your mission if you end up dead! Get out of there. Stop fooling around at this stupid auction and leave the girl alone."

"I can't," I say.

"You can, leave. Stop thinking with your fucking cock for once."

I frown. "This isn't about my cock, and you know it. If I leave now, everyone will suspect I'm the murderer, and Titus will no longer trust me."

"Fine, but keep a low profile and tell me what the hell's going on when you get a chance."

"You can trust me to do this, Gage."

He sighs. "I know—we're just so close. So fucking close..."

"I know, and I want this as badly as you do. As Lennox does. As we all do. I'm not going to fuck it up."

I end the call and then rip the knife out of my chest before thinking twice. Blood begins to gush out, but I grab a washcloth and apply pressure before picking up my shirt and tying it tight around my chest.

My shirt quickly soaks with my own blood but then stops. I won't bleed out. I need to get the wound cleaned and stitched up as soon as possible, but I have something more important to worry about first.

I yank on my pants and then start running. Scanning the hallway, there's no sign of Lilith.

Where would she have gone? If she was smart, she'd have left. She'd be in hiding or have whoever she's working with rescue her and send her far away.

But she's too stubborn for that. She went back; I know she did. She's back in that room, even if it risks the others figuring out what she did and eventually killing her for it.

I hope I'm wrong, but I have to go back too to prevent anyone from thinking I had anything to do with this.

My mind races with a hundred questions as I head back to the top floor. When I step into an elevator, an older couple looks at me—my blood-soaked shirt, naked torso, and sweat-drenched hair. The man lifts his nose in disgust as he grabs his wife and yanks her off the elevator before the door closes.

I snicker as they leave. The hotel management is going to be in a spin trying to keep their guests happy while not kicking us out. We give them too much money and business for them not to allow us to stay, though, even with all the blood and murders.

The doors open again on the top floor, and I spot her. She's still wrapped in a towel, and her ear is pressed against the door, listening to the conversations inside.

I walk silently toward her. Soon I'm standing so close that I could throw her over my shoulder and get her out of here before she even has a chance to scream.

"So you survived," she says without looking at me.

I chuckle. "You knew I would."

Her eyes cut back to mine, and I gasp at how fucking beautiful she looks. Murder is in her eyes, her red hair is drying in wild, frizzy curls, and her lips are frowning like she's incapable of smiling ever.

She shrugs, pretending she didn't deliberately stab me exactly where she did.

"What is your plan now, murderous one?" I ask.

"So they died? Good."

I nod, watching as her eyes take in my naked torso and study the shirt on my chest.

She sighs. "Turn around."

"Why, so you can stab me in the back too?"

"Just do it."

I turn and feel her hands against my back. She undoes the shirt before jerking and tying it so hard that my body lurches back, and a hiss pushes between my clenched teeth.

"There, now you won't bleed out."

"Worried about your body count?" I tease, trying to not

think about the agony in my chest. Instead, I'm thankful but confused as to why she cares that I don't die.

She rolls her eyes at me.

Who trained her? What is her goal? I want to ask all the questions, but I don't. They don't seem important right now.

She shakes her head at me. "Even being stabbed in the chest won't wipe that smirk off your face."

"Nope, nothing will stop me from having a good time. Life's too short not to enjoy every second of it. And being stabbed by you seems like an honor."

She works her jaw as if my words hurt her, but she doesn't say anything.

"So, what's your plan now? If you go back in there, they might kill you if they realize what you did. And even if they haven't figured it out yet, you're still going to have to endure an old man's dick in your mouth, a sick bastard's tongue on your cunt, and eventually a cock slamming into your pussy so hard that you'll never want to fuck again after. And that's before they decide to marry you off like you have no say in the matter."

Her lips finally curve up. "Good."

My eyes meet her blazing green ones. There's so much passion and retribution in them. She hates the Retribution Kings for something that happened, but she has the heart of one. It's clear to me this is all for revenge.

I'm guessing she's doing this all on her own, since it's such a personal vendetta. Still, someone has to know what she's doing. Someone had to have taught her how.

"So that's your plan? Let every man who bids use you, and then you'll kill them? Are you not worried they'll figure out who's doing all the killing?"

"I don't care, but I don't think they will. I'll be careful.

And I—a meek, shy, poor girl—couldn't possibly pick them off one by one. Their egos are too big to ever believe that."

She's probably right, but it's a big risk she's taking. Someone else will figure it out. It can't be a coincidence that the two men dead were the two men that won her firsts. And with that many men in the room when she stabbed them, someone must have seen her do it.

"Let me help you."

Her head snaps in my direction. "I don't need your help. I didn't need you to carry me out like a fucking damsel in distress. Clearly, I wasn't in distress. I was the killer."

I grin at her. "I know you don't need my help. You clearly have the skills and motivation to let every man bid on you and then slowly pick us all off. I know you're capable of continuing your plan, but you don't have to. I can help you."

She shakes her head.

"I make a great number two; just ask my friend Lennox or Titus."

She scoffs. "Lennox, the mafia Corsi leader? And Titus, the new current Retribution Kings leader? You work for them, and yet I'm supposed to believe that you could cross them?"

"I didn't say I would cross them, just that I would help you."

"Why?"

"Why?" I pause, trying to decide how much to bend the truth. As she squats on the floor next to me, wrapped in nothing but a towel, her red hair growing larger by the second on top of her head, and the truth that she stabbed me only to injure, the only words I can speak are the truth.

"Because I'm in love with you, murderous one. I fell in love the second I saw you. And then I fell even harder when your lips landed on mine. My pulse raced when your first began to be sold off. My blood boiled when Daniel kissed you. Fear overtook me when I heard the gunfire and thought you were dead. And when you stabbed me but didn't kill me, my heart fell completely in love with you." My grin creeps up my face.

"I know it's crazy. I barely know you and you me. And I don't expect you to share any of the feelings that I have, but I can't not help you. You, Lilith Hart, are the person for me. I know it deep in my soul."

She pauses for a long time. I don't know how she'll respond to my confession of love, seemingly out of nowhere. She works her jaw—possibly to keep from smiling herself. Finally, she says, "Prove it. Prove that you love me. That you're on my side and against the Retribution Kings. Prove that you're loyal to me above everyone else, then we can talk about your confession."

My eyes blaze. "Deal."

I want to put Lilith above everyone—Titus, Lennox, Gage...the list goes on. Hopefully, I'll never have to choose between them. I can be on her side, protecting her and helping her, while doing what I came here to do for Titus and for the others. I'm the most loyal friend, and that's not going to stop now, even for love.

CHAPTER 14

Lilith

HAYES'S CONFESSION of love takes me back. It takes everything in me to keep my mouth from falling open at his words.

He loves me.

Who confesses that when they haven't even gone on a date? When they don't even know what my favorite food is or how I like to fuck in bed? Or how we are at all compatible?

We're not—we're not fucking compatible. He's a ray of sunshine, and I'm a dark raincloud about to strike lightning.

Murderous one—I smirk at his nickname for me. I like it.

And yet his confession doesn't do anything to melt my cold heart. It doesn't convince me that he even actually loves me. Hayes seems like the kind of guy that has said I love you to every woman he sinks his cock into or wants to sink his cock into.

Hayes grabs my forearm.

My instinct is to immediately twist out of his hold and stab him again for daring to touch me. But there is also an electric charge where he touches me, and it makes me wish I had stayed in that hotel room to see where things took us.

"Trust me," he says, his crooked grin growing larger until his dimple strikes in his cheek, and my core warms at the sight of it.

"If you betray me, I'll kill you," I respond.

Hayes chuckles. "Many men have said the same to me, but the words falling from your lips are the first time I actually believe them."

"Good, you should." At yet, for some reason, when given the chance, I didn't actually kill him. *Strange*. Maybe I do think there is hope for Hayes, that he's not a monster like everyone else here.

Hayes leads me back into the penthouse, and a hush instantly falls over everyone as we step into the living room. I'm standing in only a towel. Hayes is in only his pants with his shirt wrapped around his chest wound. We look like hell.

My eyes scan the room to find the men don't look much better. I bounce from man to man, taking it all in. The wide stares, tense jawlines, furrowed brows, dripping sweat, blood-stained shirts...and then I see the bodies. Three bodies lying on the floor, covered in thin white sheets.

I only killed two of them. *Someone else killed the third.*

It takes everything in me not to smirk at the carnage and fear I created. That these brawny men who kill every day like death means nothing are actually afraid of me. They don't even yet know I was the one that caused this, but they will soon enough.

"Where the hell have you been?" says a hairy man with large biceps and a gash above his forehead, barreling toward Hayes.

Hayes still has a grip on my forearm, and he doesn't flinch as the man approaches. Instead, an annoyed grin creeps across Hayes's face.

"Really, Leo? You're going to pick a fight now? We all

need to stick together to figure out who did this," Hayes says.

Leo doesn't let Hayes's words stop him. "We already know who attacked us—it's fucking you!"

The man throws a punch, and Hayes easily dodges it. Still, Hayes doesn't let go of me.

"Stop this, Leo. I'm not your enemy. I already proved that when I was reinitiated."

My eyebrows jump up. *He was reinitiated? What task was he given?*

I shiver, thinking of my own initiation and having to go through that again. Hayes has completed two initiations—the trauma that must follow him wherever he goes. My heart aches for him for just a second before I remember that he willingly came back. He was free, and he chose to come back. He says he's on my side, not the Retribution Kings', but I'm not sure.

"Then where the hell were you?" Leo looks like he wants to pommel Hayes into the ground. But as I scan the room, no one else is jumping to Leo's aid in attacking Hayes.

Interesting.

They all hate him. They are as suspicious as I am about Hayes's loyalty. *So why aren't they taking this opportunity to take Hayes out?*

"I was ensuring Lilith was safe, while you all took out the enemy. But now it's clear I shouldn't have left you to figure that out on your own."

That gets others clenching their fists and glaring in Hayes's direction. But still, no one other than Leo approaches us.

"How do we know it wasn't you?" Leo asks.

Hayes sighs in exhaustion, as if explaining to a kindergartener why the sky is blue.

"I wasn't in the room when the attack happened. I was playing poker." Hayes begins loosening the shirt wrapped around the wound on his chest. When the gash is visible, he continues.

"And when I went in to rescue Lilith, I was stabbed. It wasn't me, and you know it. You just don't like me, so you want it to be me and think this is a good opportunity to dump on me."

No one responds to that.

"I'm going to have Colton stitch me up while you all figure out who the attacker was." Hayes leads me toward a chair pushed against the wall. I assumed he's going to take a seat, but he gently pushes me down into the chair.

"Where are your clothes?" Hayes asks me. His green eyes demand that I answer.

"The bedroom down the hall," I reply.

Hayes looks to Colton. "Get Lilith some clothes to cover her up. Then get the medical kit from the kitchen and stitch me up."

"Of course, boss," Colton says.

"Boss?" I cock an eyebrow at Hayes. He just shrugs in response.

I'm beginning to think I really don't know the man at all. He exudes confidence and leadership, even though, to my knowledge, he doesn't lead anything. And he could have easily just been killed by Leo or any of the men if they chose to take him out. He didn't break a sweat, though. His heart didn't even beat faster. And he's losing a lot of blood still from the wound I caused. He isn't in his strongest state to fight anyone.

Still, I don't say any of that out loud.

Colton returns with an oversized shirt and leggings for me and the medical kit for Hayes.

Hayes takes the clothes out of Colton's hand and then stands in front of me, blocking me from anyone else's view.

He slips the T-shirt over my head.

"Arms in," he says.

I put my arms in, and he shimmies the shirt down over my body, covering me completely before removing the towel. Even though most of the men here have already seen me naked or will soon enough.

He then kneels between my legs with the leggings. He places one of my feet in the hole of the legging and begins to pull them up.

A warmth of electricity zips through me at his touch. And as he places my second foot in the leggings and begins to pull them up my thighs, my hand grasps onto his, stopping him before I do something stupid like beg him to fuck me right here, right now.

What the hell is wrong with me?

He just touched my thigh. It's just because I haven't ever fucked a man. And being around a hot guy, knowing he could bid on me, take my virginity, make me his wife, and ruin all my plans has me panting for him to do just that. It's just hormones and biology. It doesn't mean anything; I don't have any real feelings. I just want to be fucked—and not by any of the disgusting men who I want to kill.

I want to be fucked by Hayes. And then maybe slit his throat afterward. He's still a Retribution King, after all.

I quickly yank my leggings up, putting an end to our contact.

Peter walks over, his gaze fixated on Hayes's shoulder. "You should see a doctor for your shoulder. No one here has enough medical experience to ensure you heal properly and don't get an infection."

Hayes stares Peter down. It's clear Peter isn't concerned

about Hayes's health. For some reason, Peter wants to get rid of him.

"I trust Colton to do a fine job stitching me up. And I'll make sure to see a doctor tomorrow, but thanks for your concern." Hayes flashes his signature grin, but there's a warning in his eyes as he looks at Peter.

I bite my bottom lip to keep from smiling myself as Peter nods before looking at me. "We'll start the next auction in five minutes. We don't want whoever attacked us to win. If it was an ill-fated attempt to stop the auctions, it won't work. The auctions will happen."

Peter turns before I have a chance to speak. My hands fist at my side as I glare at the back of his balding gray head.

"Down, girl. You'll get your chance to hurt him. You'll get your chance to hurt everyone here, but you have to be patient. You can't attack them again so quickly. They'll figure it out and take you captive before you have the chance to finish them," Hayes whispers in my ear.

I stare at Peter, who stops and talks to Leo. Both men stare at me with a suspicious look. They both know—or at least suspect me.

I roll my shoulders back. "They know."

"It doesn't matter if they do or don't. They have no evidence. No reason to rally the others against you—yet."

I swallow, realizing how foolish my plan was.

"Boss, I should stitch you up," Colton says.

Hayes nods, not taking his eyes off of me.

I get up from my chair. "Sit here."

Hayes shakes his head, but I don't let him refuse. "Sit," I repeat.

He sits, while I stand a few feet away, hugging my oversized shirt to my face as I think through my options and how this will all end.

Colton pulls up another chair and makes quick work of Hayes's shoulder. I should be planning my next move, but my eyes are fixated on his shoulder. How his muscles contract with every breath he takes. How his long hair has fallen out of his bun in long, dark curls. How his green eyes watching me sets fire between my legs in a blaze of arousal I don't know how to extinguish.

Colton finishes, and I stare at his work. The gash I opened in his chest is now closed by stitches. Hayes didn't once wince or hiss or make a single sound. *What pain has the man endured to not be affected by being stitched up? Does it match my own?*

Suddenly, four men surround me. Four Retribution Kings. Blocking my view of Hayes and the rest of the room.

My heart pounds in my chest, and I instinctually grab for a weapon on my body, but I don't have one. I have nothing. And as skilled as I am, I can't fight off four armed men while I have nothing.

"What is this?" I ask.

They don't answer. My arms are yanked viciously behind my back, and metal snaps around my wrists. My feet are lifted off the floor as more metal rubs against my ankles. A blindfold is tightened over my eyes, and I'm completely at their disposal. They could do anything they wanted to me, and I would be powerless to stop them.

"Peter! What the hell is this? This wasn't part of the contract! I'm a Retribution King, same as any man in this room. I'm initiated. I signed a contract to sell my firsts and myself into marriage. I didn't sign up for whatever twisted game this is!"

I don't expect an answer, but I refuse to stay silent and not fight back, even if it risks everything.

Peter answers, though. "The contract you signed allows

me to do whatever I want to you. *I* own you until your future husband buys you, and then *he'll* own you. You aren't a Retribution King—you're the future wife of one. And because of you, the Retribution Kings are now under attack. Someone wants you. Someone is fighting for you. You can't be trusted, and you're not worth men dying over."

CHAPTER 15

Lilith

I ALWAYS KNEW the Retribution Kings were monsters. I knew the truth from a young age, even before they did anything to personally hurt me or my family. They always acted like they were the ones who would right any wrong, would restore balance when some evil was committed. But they were the evil all along.

I knew I would die fighting them, but I hoped my family would live. I hoped my sisters would live and escape this life. It wasn't supposed to end this way.

I've sat in a dark dungeon for days with barely any food or water. No one has spoken to me. No one has said a word to me. No one has said they know I'm the one who killed two of their own, and I'm about to be punished for my crimes. I'm most likely about to be tortured, raped, and then killed.

I just have to stop them from seeking retribution against my family. They had nothing to do with this.

But I can't stop anything from a cage.

And Hayes—he said he loved me, the foolish man. But he clearly doesn't care if he can't save me from this fate.

My wrists and ankles are still locked together in cuffs, and I still have a blindfold over my eyes. Suddenly I hear the metal door of my cage open.

"It's time," a deep man's voice says.

I don't respond. Maybe if I die with dignity, they'll let my family go. That's all I care about now. It's all I should have ever cared about—earning enough money for them to live, not getting retribution. I thought I could do both—I was wrong.

I feel rough hands on my biceps and thighs as I'm lifted up again. Up, up, up my body is carried up a set of stairs.

"Where are you taking me?" I ask, unable to keep silent.

"To your new owner."

Owner.

Fuck them all.

I don't care if they kill me; I'll find a way to come back from the dead and kill them all.

I'm tossed into the back of a van. Doors are slammed shut, and I'm once again left with doing nothing but waiting and waiting and waiting.

The van drives quickly, but I have no idea what's happening or why. No idea what they discovered or decided to do with me in the days I've been locked in a cage and forgotten. No idea what was in that fucking contract that makes them think they can do this to me.

Who am I kidding? Contract or not, they can do whatever they want to me. Who would stop them?

My eyes drift closed from the bouncing of the van as we drive.

"Wake up, sleeping beauty. You don't want to miss the look on your new master's face when he sees you. I don't know who you really are, Lilith Hart, but I do know you're a much stronger spirit than you first let on. And he's going to enjoy breaking your will and making you into what you were always meant to be," a man says.

The voice sounds an awful lot like Leo. At least that must mean Leo's not my new owner.

I'm roughly yanked out of the van. I try to fight, try to break free of the handcuffs, try to wiggle the blindfold off my face so I can see—but nothing works.

"Stop struggling, or we'll drug you," Leo says.

I still.

I should save my energy anyway for the moment when someone decides I'm tame enough to remove these cuffs. It will be their last mistake when they do—I'll take no mercy.

I feel the hands on me relax as I stop struggling. Finally, they stop walking.

"I'm going to enjoy watching him break you, whore. He does like to share his toys after they're trained," Leo says.

I turn my head and sink my teeth into his flesh. I'm not sure what body part I bit, but I don't let go until I taste the metallic of his blood.

"You fucking bitch!"

My body lands with a thump on the floor before a sharp kick lands against my ribs.

I gasp at the shock of agony shooting through my body.

My hair is yanked back. "They all think you're a plant one of our enemies put in our ranks, and someday they'll come to your rescue. But I think they're wrong. No one is coming to your rescue. You're a nobody. And you'll soon learn how vicious we can truly be. You should have continued living in that podunk two-bedroom trailer. You could have spent your life sucking cock for money to survive. Instead, you thought you could play the hero. We aren't the reason you're poor—your father is. And you're the reason your sisters will remain poor."

"Leave them alone!" I shout.

I can feel his smile against my cheek. "I will. They aren't the one I want." His tongue licks up my cheek, and I shiver away. "You are."

"Enjoy your time with your new master. Soon enough, I'll get my chance with you. Be prepared—you're going to need every ounce of strength to survive me."

And then I'm alone to wait for my new owner. A man who bought me, who plans to break me.

If not Leo, then who?

Leo's words haunt me as I wait. And wait and wait.

I can't see through the blindfold. My wrists and ankles are bound, and I don't try to fight it. Whoever bought me just sealed their fate. Buying me will be the last thing they ever do. As soon as I'm sure my family has the money, I'll kill them. And then I'll take down as many Retribution Kings as I can before I go.

"I didn't think they'd actually manage to deliver you." My heart stops at the sound of his voice. He chuckles. "At least not without you taking off a few of their fingers first."

My heart does a little somersault, but I refuse to smile at Hayes's voice. I should feel relieved—I don't.

"Tell me you at least drew some blood, murderous one?" I feel his breath on my neck, so he must have lowered down to the floor where I lay. And yet, he hasn't touched me. He hasn't removed any of the handcuffs or blindfold.

"I bit Leo," I say.

He chuckles fiercely. "Good, the bastard deserves so much more."

His thumb brushes up my jawline and then slides the blindfold off the top of my head. His face is an inch above mine, and when our eyes meet, I gasp.

My steel-caged heart, the heart I've kept locked away, the heart that turned into vengeance before I was even old enough to ever let a man into my life—*that heart*—throbs.

Thump-thump.
Thump-thump.
Thump-thump.

It beats as if calling for him, knowing something I don't. This man is the man it's been searching for without my knowing that it was searching at all. This man is the one who could make me smile when all I want to do is frown. This man is the one who I could share my destiny with, my pain with, my everything with.

This man.

What is it about this man that my heart instantly trusts him?

Is it because he saved you, twice now?

Leo could have bought me. A worse man could have. They could have tortured me until they learned the truth of what happened. That I killed those men without thinking of the consequences. That I risked everything for retribution.

This man didn't allow me to suffer that fate.

This man loves me.

This man is my sunshine, my hope, my only chance at loving again.

His gorgeous smile drops. His eyes flick over my face, concerned something's wrong.

"Lilith? Are you—"

I don't let him finish his sentence. I press my lips against his.

I don't think. For once, I follow my heart instead of my need for revenge.

His lips don't hesitate for a second the moment I press mine against his. Both our eyes stay open on each other as we part our lips simultaneously.

Our tongues press into each other, sweeping without any hesitation. It feels like so much more than I remember. He kisses like he doesn't have a care in the world. It's like all he's thinking about is me in this moment, and this is all he could ever want.

I desperately try to match him to let go of all the heartache I've endured. I kiss away the pain. I kiss away the feeling of my life only being about one thing. I kiss him like he's the only thing that matters in the world.

Hayes makes it easy. He opens his soul to me with each kiss, and his body gently presses against mine until I can feel all of him as his hand strokes my hip. But he doesn't take anything further. He doesn't rip my clothes off or slide his hand underneath. He doesn't force me to do anything when he easily could. I'm still handcuffed, and as Leo said—he owns me.

Leo's words come back to me. *"I'm going to enjoy watching him break you, whore. He does like to share his toys after they're trained..."*

Have I gotten Hayes all wrong? Is he the kind of guy who lures women in with his charming smile and easygoing demeanor, only to break them and then share them with all his buddies?

I stop the kiss abruptly.

Hayes stops the second I do. He doesn't ask what the kiss, or the sudden end to the kiss, was about. He doesn't push me.

"No one ever taught you how to get out of handcuffs?" Hayes asks.

"No one ever taught me anything. Everything I've learned, I taught myself."

He looks at me with an intensity I haven't seen on his face before. The playfulness is gone, replaced with sorrow that ripples through me. Then, in a flash, he's back to grinning.

"Well, consider this a free lesson." He reaches into the

hair beneath the bun on top of his head and pulls out a bobby pin.

I raise my eyebrows at him.

He chuckles at my expression. "Always carry a bobby pin in your hair. It has many uses, and you never know when you need one."

He places it in one of my hands.

"Now remove the tips and then straighten it."

I do as he says.

"Good, now bend one end at a 90-degree angle and then see if you can get it into the lock."

It takes me a few tries to get the metal end into the lock, but I finally succeed.

"The next part is where you need patience."

"I'm patient. You don't think I'm patient?"

He laughs. "No, murderous one, you aren't patient. If you were patient, then Daniel and Harvey would still be alive. You wouldn't be in this mess, and you'd have a plan to kill all of them at once."

I frown. "I'm patient." I insert the bobby pin into the lock and swirl it around, trying to force the lock to open.

Hayes gives me a knowing look, but he doesn't criticize me.

Frustration boils beneath my skin as my wrists scrape against the metal. I've broken free of restraints before, but always by manipulating my wrist to create space for my hand to get free. I've never picked a lock.

I wince as the metal digs into my skin. Hayes's fingers move over mine, stilling me.

My heart races rapidly in my chest. Wordlessly and slowly, he guides my fingers until, finally, the latch pops free. Hayes removes his fingers from mine and sits back, allowing me to remove the other handcuff from my wrist.

My shoulders slump in relief the second I have free range of my arms again.

He waits without a sound while I remove the handcuffs from my ankles, using the technique he just taught me.

I should thank him, but I don't. I can't yet. He's saved me multiple times, but I can't thank him. I don't trust him enough for that yet.

There's something he's hiding. There's some truth he needs to tell me before I can thank him. Before I can trust him. Before I can admit that I might love him.

"You bought me?" I snap, my words coming out harsher and more accusatory than I meant for them to.

"Would you have rathered Leo or someone else to have bought you?"

"Yes!"

He blinks as if I slapped him.

I stand up, not liking having this conversation while I'm in a position of weakness on the floor. Then I'm eye to eye with Hayes.

"Why? Because you like pain that much? If Leo bought you, you wouldn't escape. You couldn't even get free of handcuffs; he'd use far more restraints if you were his."

"Because I can't kill you!" I yell, breathless.

Hayes's eyes widen, and then he grins. "You can."

"I can't."

He takes my hands in his. "You can. And someday, you'll realize that. If you need to, you kill me. You put yourself first —always. I'm not a man worth saving, protecting, or stopping you from doing what you have to do. Do you understand? Promise me you won't hesitate to kill me when the time comes."

I glare at him. "No. I don't make promises like that. Not anymore."

He sighs. "Fine, but if you realize someday that you want to kill me, then do it."

"You have that much of a death wish?"

He shrugs. "I'm not afraid of death. I've lived a good life. I have good friends. I live every moment like it's my last. And I love you. I can't even explain why, just that I know that I do. Whether you ever love me back or not doesn't matter. I want you to be happy. I want you to get to live because I know your life hasn't had much happiness. And if killing me means you'll finally be able to be who you were always meant to be, then I want you to kill me, Lily."

My heart stills as he calls me Lily. No one has ever called me that before, but I kind of like it.

Fuck, I'm so totally fucked.

"So you bought out my contract? Or did you just buy my next first?" I ask.

Hayes hesitates, his smile faltering.

"The contract is over. You have a new contract. The auction is over. The money will all be sent to your family. And you'll be married to a monster in a few weeks."

"You're not a monster."

He looks at me with a look dripping with so much pain that all I want to do is wrap my arms around him until he smiles again. The world isn't right if Hayes isn't smiling.

"I am—and I'm sorry for that, Lily. But at least I'm a monster who will help you get revenge before you finally decide I'm worth stabbing in the heart."

CHAPTER 16

Hayes

TIME IS RUNNING OUT. I need to find Ruby. I need to fulfill my part of our plan. I need to figure out my Titus problem. My phone is buzzing with relentless calls from Gage. And there's a missed call from an unknown number, which I suspect was Lennox risking everything by calling me.

And instead of dealing with any of my problems, I'm showing Lilith a tour of the mansion I brought her to.

She looks suspiciously around every room, like she's waiting to be surprised by a Retribution King I've kept hidden to attack her.

As strong and as capable as she is, she's equally afraid. The skills she's picked up are all a defense mechanism. It's something to protect her from the constant fear and trauma coursing through her veins.

We stop in the kitchen, which has a full array of professional-grade appliances and pans that I'm dying to use.

"What can I make you to eat?" I ask.

She raises her eyebrow at me and looks around the room. "You don't have a chef on staff?"

I chuckle at that. "No, I don't. I don't have any hired help."

A bewildered look crosses her face. "You can't be serious. How do you clean, and cook, and keep up with this house without help?"

"Cleaning isn't hard when you only use one or two rooms, and cooking I enjoy."

"I don't believe that you can cook more than a grilled cheese."

I give her a devious grin. "Sit down and watch the master work."

Twenty minutes later, I've made her the best damn grilled cheese she's ever had, complete with a side of tomato bisque soup.

"Holy shit," she stares at me with instant love in her eyes.

I chuckle, but then I'm used to that reaction. It's what I do well. I cook, I please people, I make them grin in their darkest moments.

"You really weren't kidding. This is the best thing I've ever tasted."

I nod, watching her as she takes another bite of her grilled cheese. A soft moan escapes her lips, making my cock harden.

I want her. I want her more than fucking anything. I want to tell her everything, but I can't. And after spending a couple of days apart while I figured out how to buy her away from those monsters, I realized the truth. I realized our truth and how this is going to fucking end.

There is no hope for me. It doesn't matter if I complete my mission or not. It doesn't matter what Titus decides. It doesn't matter even if I make her fall in love with me these next couple of days. She's going to hate me in the end for all the lies. There is no amount of love that will overcome the pain she'll feel when she learns the truth.

Yet, I can't tell her. I can't save us all the trouble now. I can't stop my heart from clinging to the tiniest bit of hope that something will change between now and whenever she finds out.

"What are you thinking about, *master*?" she asks.

I blink, realizing that I've tuned out while she ate the rest of her food.

"What did you just call me?"

"Master. Or do you prefer owner or sir?"

I stare at her, blank-faced.

She chuckles. "You bought me, right? So what do you want me to call you? What room are you going to lock me up in? Or what part of this massive mansion am I allowed in? Who are my guards? You know, give me my orders."

Her eyes are wide and unruly. Her words have a bite to them. As much as she's grateful that I'm the one who bought her over the others, she's still mad that this is the world she's in. But I don't want her thinking that—any of that. We're on the same side, her and me. Even when the truth gets out, and she thinks we're not.

"I don't own you," I say sternly.

She turns on the stool at the counter and faces me as I sit next to her. "But you do. You signed a contract and paid my family millions to own me."

I shake my head. I take her hand and place it against my chest, next to the spot where she stabbed me, over my heart.

"Feel that heartbeat. Feel it racing under your touch. You do that to me." She sucks in a breath. "I signed a contract and paid millions, when I should have been running as far away from you as possible. You weren't in my plan. In fact, you'll make my goals so much harder to accomplish. But I couldn't leave you alone. I don't own you—you own me, Lilith."

My head dips down at the same time hers curves up, and our mouths find each other again. Hunger fills my body as her soft lips touch mine. An uncontrollable desire rips through me, and my hands grip her waist. Before I realize what I'm doing, I'm pulling her onto my lap. Her legs straddle me as her hands grip the sides of my face.

She deepens the kiss as her body begins to rock on my lap. Every part of my body hardens beneath her. I can't control my hands as they race up and down her hips to the bottom curve of her breasts. I want to touch so much more, and if she keeps this up, I'm going to.

She grinds against me again, and the moan I let out rips through the room. It's been too long since I've let a woman ride me. And I've never wanted to be owned by a woman as I do now.

I pull my lips from hers as she continues to try to kiss me. "Lily, we need to talk first. Then I'll fuck you every way you want if you still want me to."

Her lips are swollen, and her eyes are dazed. I'm not even sure if she heard me speak or not.

I smile softly as I run my hand through her soft red curls.

"Did you hear me?"

She nods slowly.

I pick her up and carry her to the couch in the living room, needing her off my lap if I'm going to be able to get the next words out.

When we're both seated, she says, "What do you want to talk about?"

"The contract."

"What about the contract? You own me. You're going to

marry me in a few weeks. I think we can fuck before we're married," she teases.

I shake my head. "I left out one important detail. I tried my best to remove this part, but I couldn't."

Her smile drops. "Remove what part?"

"We have to film all of your firsts. I bought them. I own them. But anyone can pay to watch. I said I'd pay the money, but—"

"Peter said no. It's not about the money. It's about the twisted enjoyment they get. And after what happened, they don't trust me."

"No, they don't. And I think they hope they can figure out who is behind the attacks by recording you. They think they can blackmail whoever you're working with into showing themselves to save you."

She pauses and processes, her eyes meeting mine. The gloom I've seen countless times in them returns. Gone is the sparkle from just a moment ago.

"It means that you can't fake it with me. You can't be gentle. You will have to play the part that is expected of you as a Retribution King. You may have bought me, but the Retribution Kings still own me."

"Yes," I say softly, hating it as much as she does. "They own us both. But we'll get our revenge; I promise you that."

"How?"

"We fulfill the contract. We get them to trust us. We find their weakness. And then we kill them all."

"Seems kind of vague."

"Let's get through the contract part without killing each other, then we'll worry about step two."

She takes a deep breath, her lips curling up. "I don't think 'getting through' is the phrase I'd use when describing having sex with you."

"No?" my smile returns. "Then what word would you use?"

"Savor—I'm going to savor our time together. I'm not going to suffer. I'm not going to 'get through' it. And I'm not going to cower and pretend I'm afraid. Not for them. I'm going to enjoy every moment with you."

She doesn't have to say the rest. She knows this thing between us has a time limit on it. She doesn't realize the whole truth yet, but she's right—I'll make sure she enjoys every moment with me.

I lean into her, nuzzling her neck. "You'll enjoy every second of it, even if to them they think you're terrified of me."

She squirms next to me. "And if I don't fulfill the contract? What if I let you fuck me right here without filming it for those sick bastards?"

"Then they'll kill us. But death might be worth it," I wink at her.

CHAPTER 17

Lilith

"WHAT'S THE NEXT FIRST?" I ask him, heat pulsing through my body. I want him to take them all right now—my virginity and every other first I can think of. I'm dripping with need for him to fuck me every way imaginable.

I may not love him like he claims he does me. I may not even care about the man that much, but my lady bits don't care. They are hungry for him like he's the only man on the planet.

As I straddle him and his sultry eyes stare into mine with a mischievous grin, all of my thoughts fall away. For months now, I've been focused on a singular goal. My life has been harsh, and I've never even thought about taking a lover to escape the pain. Never until I felt this hot-blooded man beneath me—hot and beautiful and full of promises to make me forget, if only for a moment. He may possibly even help me find a way to get revenge against the Retribution Kings. But his eyes definitely promise a good time in the bedroom, and I'll take it even if that's all he can offer me.

"Blow job," he replies.

I didn't think two words could kill my mojo so quickly.

His eyes twinkle in amusement at my reaction.

"Not what you were expecting me to say?" he asks.

I frown, my eyes drifting down his hard chest to where I'm straddling his hard cock. Sure, I want to see it, taste him, and take him deep into my mouth.

But giving him a blow job will do nothing to tamper my own arousal. If anything, it's just going to make it harder to control myself. I'm going to be writhing in painful desire until our next first, whatever and whenever that will be. I won't be able to focus on a plan for revenge.

"I promise you'll enjoy tasting my cock."

I lick my lips. "It's not that..."

He kisses just behind my ear, and heat floods my body. "It's that you need a release."

I nod. My hooded eyes meet his gaze. "I need everything. Can't we just do it all now, record everything, and be done with them? And then we won't have to think about it before the wedding."

He stills. "First of all, even though I have to film us, I'm not going to take everything at once."

"Why not?"

"Because I'm a selfish bastard that wants to enjoy every experience with you. Recording is going to take a lot out of us. And the longer I delay each recording, the longer we have to come up with a plan to get out of it at all."

His reasoning makes sense.

"Is there an order to the firsts? Like blow job has to be next?"

He shakes his head. "Not really."

I narrow my eyes. "Then why blow job?"

He chuckles lightly, his thumb moving in tantalizing circles along my hip. "Because it exposes me more than you. And I want as much time as possible to think of how to protect you when I have to record us doing more intimate things."

"Oh," my mouth falls open, and my cheeks warm. I don't know what to say. I can't believe how considerate he is. He's sweet, and kind, and loving. He did say he loved me. I still think he's mad for thinking that or doesn't realize what it means to love someone, but I'm not going to argue that point right now.

His hand reaches up, and he tucks a strand of my hair behind my ear. "Don't worry, Lily. I'll make sure you get your release without actually taking another first."

His voice sends thrills through me, trying to imagine what his words could possibly mean. But I'm too bashful to ask.

Hayes lifts me off his lap and onto my feet, his hands never leaving my body as he intertwines our fingers. I take a deep, calming breath as our hands lock together. *Why do I feel warm and safe when he's holding my hand?*

He leads me through the mansion to one of the bedrooms. "You can choose another room, but I thought you'd like this one best."

"It's the master bedroom," I say.

He nods. "Take your time. You should find anything you need in the bathroom and closet. I'm going to set everything up in the bedroom at the other end of the hall. Meet me there when you're ready." He leans in, brushing the softest of kisses against my lips, and then leaves before I can say anything.

I exhale a deep breath, tempted to follow him out of the room and tell him to hell with everything and everyone; I don't care about the risks—fuck me right now.

But the need to survive long enough to get revenge wins out. I don't know how they'd know if we fucked without recording ourselves. Or if they'd really kill us if we did, but I'll go along with Hayes's plan for now.

When I enter the bathroom and find a large free-standing tub, I decide to take advantage of it. I want to clean off everything that's happened and calm my nerves before reuniting with Hayes.

I take far longer in the tub than I initially planned. Maybe it's nerves. Maybe it's because I was wrong about my attraction toward Hayes. Maybe I find him repulsive. Maybe I don't trust him. Maybe it's because I know I'm going to enjoy this when I should want to slice through his jugular until he bleeds out.

Hayes is a Retribution King, and he has secrets.

Is he really helping me? Or is he distracting me to keep me from killing more men until they figure out what to do with me?

I push the door open to the bedroom that he told me to meet him in, my decision made.

My heart catches in my throat when I see him. He's showered and changed into a pair of tight black pants but didn't bother with a shirt. His long dark hair is pulled back into a bun that drips water onto his strong back as he bends over the bed.

He stills when I enter, feeling me even though I haven't said a word. All of my fears disappear as I step toward him. I've never wanted a man more. I don't know who Hayes is. I know virtually nothing about him. I don't know where his loyalties lie. I don't know what gets him up in the morning. But I know he's a good kisser, and he loves me.

Jesus, that word—love.

What the hell am I supposed to do with that?

He can't love me. He doesn't know me any more than I know him. He's just infatuated with me because I have a pretty face, smart mouth, and know how to use a knife and a gun. Once he gets what he wants from me and fucks me, the infatuation will fade.

But then he paid to marry me...he'll be in my life forever.

I shake my head, not letting myself go there.

Hayes turns, his broad chest and narrow waist taking my breath away.

He's mine, the words shoot through me like a possessive fire.

Fuck, I'm so screwed.

The tattoo of the Retribution Kings is marked onto his chest, slightly covered by a bandage still over the spot where I stabbed him. Glancing up, I expect to see his always-present grin and equally adorable dimple. Instead, his mouth drops when he stares at me.

I glance down at the oversized black shirt that I'm sure belongs to him. It barely covers my ass. My red hair is curling at the ends as it slowly dries. I'm not wearing any makeup, nothing to hide who I am. There's nothing special about what I'm wearing, but the way Hayes looks at me makes me feel like Cinderella descending the stairs at the ball. I've never seen a man look at me like I'm beautiful, special, *his.*

My tongue sweeps across my bottom lip. I don't care about the ridiculous and cruel circumstances that have led to this. I want this. I want him.

Desire sweeps through the room, and I feel our bodies being pushed together as if by a force we don't control.

Hayes's lips lift up into his infectious grin. That dimple caves in at his cheek as my heart does small somersaults in my chest. His eyes sparkle with a mischievousness and playfulness that only he could find in a moment like this.

I crack my own smile, unable to keep my grumpy facade up for long around him.

"Do this right," a deep voice from behind me makes me jump.

I spin to find a serious-looking man with dark brown skin, a shaved head, and a viscous look—the polar opposite of Hayes. His brows are furrowed, and his mouth curls into a sneer with an unyielding intensity that I'm glad I'm not on the other side of. He's not looking at me; he's looking at Hayes.

"You can't afford to fuck this up, Hayes. You made your choice despite my protests. You know what will happen if you don't." He turns to me, and I shudder. His predatory gaze skims over me as if he's about to pounce. And unlike Hayes, with this man, I doubt I'd enjoy it.

"You know I won't fuck this up, Gage."

Gage, that's the man's name. It fits.

His gaze sweeps over me one last time as if to determine if I'm worthy whatever price his friend will pay. I don't know what he decides, but he turns toward where I see a laptop has been set up on a small table, and my stomach curls.

"Press record when you're ready. It will be sent in real-time to the other Retribution Kings." One last glance to Hayes, and then Gage vanishes out the door.

I exhale a ragged breath, realizing I've been holding it the entire time he spoke.

"You okay? Gage isn't exactly great at social interactions. But he's all bark and no bite," Hayes says.

"You sure? It seems like he has quite a bite. What was he talking about?"

Hayes is in front of me in a second, his hands resting gently on my hips as he stares down at me with a pain in his eyes.

"That I can't save you."

"What?" my throat dries.

"I should have found another way. I should have saved you. This is..."

"You're not responsible for me, and you're definitely not responsible for saving me. I don't want you to save me. I want you to help me get revenge."

"We don't have to do this tonight. We can prolong it until we find another solution."

"No, we can't. And I don't want to."

His mouth drops open as his breathing picks up. "What do you want, Lilith? My murderous one."

"I want to suck your cock. I want you to lick me. I want to make you come and you me. I want to feel your cock sliding into me, ruining me for any other man."

His teeth grind together as his eyes smolder into darkness. There is no smile, no playfulness, only an anticipation of what's about to happen.

"You're sure?"

I nod. "Yes, I don't care about the reasons why. I want you. I trust you." At least with this. With my plans for revenge, I'm not so sure. But with my body, my pleasure—I trust him completely.

He shudders, and I haven't even touched him.

"I'm sorry. I'm sorry for what I'm about to become. But I promise I'll make it good for you."

Aren't I the one supposed to make it good for him? I open my mouth to ask, but he reaches behind me, and I know he's turning on the camera.

A fervent anticipation spreads through me. I don't have to wait long to find out what Hayes meant.

He grabs me roughly, fisting my hair in his hand. His eyes turn into dark orbs, and his lips curl into a menacing grin. He laughs manically as my eyes widen with a whisper of fear swirling in my lower belly.

He pulls me roughly to the bed, tossing me down on it until I land on my back. I instinctively climb up the bed, trying to get away from him. I look for a weapon, anything to use against him.

Dark, villainous laughter fills the room as I try to get away from him. Hayes stands at the foot of the bed, his back to the laptop as he looks at me, climbing away from him.

Trust me, he mouths with a soft smile.

This is all an act, a game. He's not going to hurt me, not going to take. And the way he's standing in front of the camera, already blocking my body from view, tells me I should trust him. The desire pooling in my belly won't let me back out. I want this. I want him.

I give him the subtlest of nods, giving him my permission to continue. *Damn, am I going to enjoy this when the wicked gleam returns to his eyes. I'm sure of it.*

CHAPTER 18

Hayes

I WILL NOT BREAK HER.

That's the promise I repeat to myself over and over in my head. *I will not break her—not today, not ever.*

However, that is what I'm meant to do—show these men her brokenness. And by the end, I'll end up breaking her heart with the truth.

But I won't break her. She'll survive; she has to.

Suddenly, I understand Lennox better, what he went through. I understand it all. Because I'd do anything for her.

I will not hurt her. Everything she feels is going to be pleasure. I got the look of fear in her eyes for the cameras. That's enough. Nothing else has to hurt her. I've caused her enough pain as it is.

I climb up the bed until I'm straddling her at the waist.

Her eyes are big and wild, her breathing ragged. I know she trusts me, but there is still a tinge of fear in her eyes.

I don't allow myself to go there. I have a job to do, and it's the only way to save us both for at least another night.

"You're going to suck my cock, Lilith. Suck until I've come deep down that pretty throat of yours."

She gasps and gives an eager nod.

"Good girl," I say as I begin to undo my pants.

Her eyes are focused on where my hands pull down the zipper of my pants until my cock springs free—hard and straining for her. It doesn't remember that this is all a game. It doesn't know we won't be hurting her or actually getting sucked, at least not here or now.

I expect a moment of shock or a slight fear at me shoving my cock down her throat. But if she has any fear, I don't see a drop of it on her face.

Her eyes darken into devilish slits, her tongue glides over her bottom lip, and her hand reaches out to my thigh as she tries to pull me toward her. She wants me, wants this.

I don't deserve her.

Nevertheless, I won't change my plan. I will not take her firsts on camera unless I have to, even if she wants me to. I'll find another way.

If it's ever found out, I'll be the one punished, not her.

"Tie her to the bed," Peter's voice from the laptop sounds behind me, as if I could ever forget that this isn't for me. This is a fucked up show that I'm participating in.

I growl, and the guys think it's because I've turned into an animal about to tie up his prey. In reality, it's the order I'm angry with, the control I'm losing.

I'd kill them all if I didn't think it was Lilith's prerogative to get to kill them first.

Two handcuffs are already secured to the bed. I knew what would be asked of me; I just hoped I wouldn't have to do it.

Lilith gives me the slightest of winks, and then I attack. Grabbing her arms, I yank them viciously above her head while she writhes and struggles beneath me.

I admit, my cock hardens, feeling her pretend to struggle

against me and knowing it's all a show. She's pretending as much as I am.

She doesn't want them to see her as weak, so I'm surprised she's going along with this. I thought for sure she'd refuse to act afraid, but she's enjoying the game.

As one of her hands is clasped into a handcuff, the other strikes against my cheek. I growl on instinct, my breath hot on her neck.

"There's my murderous one," I whisper so only she can hear.

Her face pinks, and her eyes hood. *Fuck me, I want her.* It's going to take everything in me not to do this for real. I secure her second wrist until both are above her head, while her legs are still pinned under my hips.

"You know I could get free if I wanted to," she whispers.

"Good thing you don't want to," I breathe back.

Then I yank her head back as I climb up her body, brushing my pierced cock against her lips.

"Open, Lilith," I say, purposefully not using any nicknames I have for her on camera.

She opens wide, ready for me—for all of me.

I almost take what she's offering. At the last moment, I slide down her cheek instead of her mouth, shuddering as I imagine what it would be like for her lips to be circling me as I slide inside her. It doesn't take much imagination.

There's some grumbling about the shitty view and changing the camera angle, but I don't listen to them. I know they can't see shit, and I don't care.

I won't do this on camera. I won't do any of it. I won't hurt her. I won't take anything. Damn the consequences for me if it means saving her from everything.

Her eyebrows lift in a questioning gaze.

I grab her throat, my eyes swirling with the darkness inside me. Darkness she will never have to experience. Darkness I will take with me long after she kills me. I won't let anyone kill me but her.

"Take me deeper. Take all of me, Lilith."

She pretends to gag on my cock, finally agreeing to this act.

I didn't know if I was going to fuck her mouth for real or not until I hit record, but now I know the risks I'll take for her. I won't hurt her. I won't break her. I won't even fuck her. I should have never told her I love her—that was my biggest mistake.

I have no idea how I can make her think I hate her. It's not possible, so I'm fucking screwed. But as I fake come into the pillow instead of her throat, I know I didn't break her. I breathed life into her and gave her another reason to want to murder these men.

CHAPTER 19

Lilith

SILENCE SUFFOCATES me as we walk back to my bedroom. Hayes is only wearing his pants, and I'm still in the oversized black shirt hanging down to my mid-thighs. We pause at my bedroom door, and I spin to face him, finding him already walking away without a word.

"What was that?" I spit out. My words are angrier than I intended, but Hayes lied to me. He could have told me he was going to fake everything. He could have had me blow him for real. My cheeks flush with red, hot desire for him.

Jesus, I've never been so turned on. I'm practically panting as I stare at his shirtless body and remember how fucking gorgeous his cock was. Long and thick and veiny. And the piercing at the tip—I wanted to run my tongue up the length of him and over that pierced tip. I wanted to feel the control of watching him shatter beneath my touch.

"Protecting you—that was protecting you!" Hayes growls.

I know he was protecting me. I know he was keeping the cameras, the eyes, the disgusting men on the other side of that laptop from seeing me and getting their sick pleasure. I know it, but him protecting me doesn't give me what I want, what I need.

"I never asked you to protect me!" I shout back, unable to get out any reasonable words through the heat swept over my body.

All I want is him.

All I see is him.

I'm drowning in flaming carnal lust, and I have no idea how to put out the fire without his help.

I run my hand through my hair as I pace my room, trying to keep from looking at Hayes. I can't think clearly when I'm thinking about him.

Why would he do this?

"I love you, Lilith. I had to protect you. I thought I could handle making it enjoyable for you and for that to be enough protection. But I can't—I can't put you through any of that. I can't let them watch. I can't."

Desperation fills the air between us. We're needy for many different things, but there's one thing we're each craving. We're desperate for each other.

"You can't protect me from this. Not forever. Not again. I heard them speaking. They were furious they didn't have a better view. You can't fake it again without them punishing you."

"I don't care," Hayes growls.

I jump at that deep-seated rage in his voice. But a moment later, I'm walking toward him anyway.

Hayes grabs onto the doorframe, keeping himself planted to the spot. He's not coming in, but not leaving either.

I stop in front of him, using all the control in my body to not jump on his body, wrap my legs around his waist, and force him to fuck me. Each of our self-control is teetering on the edge of exploding.

His nostrils flare as he glares down at me with both hunger and fury. Deep, slow breaths burn through his lungs.

Want, so much fucking want for each other.

Love is what Hayes would call it.

I can't think of a word that accurately describes this painful, controlling feeling that's suffocating me into submission.

"Is it just your love for me that's protecting me, or is there something else?" I ask as I stare up at Hayes with hooded eyes.

His eyes dart away for a split second. He loves me, but there's something else he's not telling me—some other reason.

I can never love him. He's hiding too much, and I still don't fully trust where his loyalties lie. *To the Retribution Kings, to the Corsi mafia, or to me?*

His breathing is fast and deep as his chest rises and falls in rapid succession. His eyes have turned into dark orbs, and pain is etched into his features.

I reach my hand up and stroke his cheek. Needing to comfort him, but also just needing him. His eyes squeeze shut at my touch, and he shudders.

"Kiss me," I whisper. We need to kiss, to let our bodies decide our fate.

"Murderous one," Hayes says with a warning in his tone, but I don't heed it.

I press my lips to his, half expecting him to throw me off of him and tell me to go to bed. But the second my lips brush against his, he yields to me, as if he knew how this was going to end all along. He doesn't touch me, but the hunger in his actions, as he splits my lips open and sweeps his tongue into my mouth, tells me he's one second away from losing all control.

The kiss is torture for me. Even though I can sense him

losing control, I'm not sure I can persuade him to take this any further. Something changed between the last time we made out and now, *but what?*

Hayes breaks away, sucking my bottom lip in his mouth until the very last second before releasing me.

"Please," I whimper. "I want you, Hayes. I don't care about the rest."

Hayes studies me closely. Slowly, his sinister grin returns to his face, and I can finally take a breath. Whatever was controlling him before is gone from his mind.

"You're going to regret begging me, murderous one."

I shake my head, my chest rising and falling as I wait for him to strike. He will, and being with him will probably change my life. But it won't change my goals, my future, or my fate—nor his.

We're both doomed to sacrifice ourselves in the name of revenge. That much is clear, so we might as well enjoy ourselves before our end comes.

"I'll regret nothing," I purr back with a dark expression on my face.

I'm lifted into the air before I even register my next breath. My head and back slam onto the top of the memory foam bed.

Hayes's green eyes swirl as he stares at my body. "I've wanted to do this since I saw you across that ballroom."

"I hate to admit that I've only recently wanted this."

His body hovers over mine as his teeth nip at my bottom lip. "I'm not."

He sweeps my hair to one side as his lips travel down my jawline to my exposed neck. As he kisses the tender spots, flames fan through my body in a way I've never felt before.

His hand travels up my thigh as he pushes the shirt up my body, exposing my black panties. His touch overwhelms my senses, and for a moment, I'm frozen beneath him. He kisses the palm of my hand, relaxing my nerves and encouraging me to explore his body.

I tangle my hand in his hair, pulling him tightly to me. His eyes seer into me from beneath his glasses, and my cheeks pinken.

"You're so gorgeous, Lilith. Everything I'm about to do is because we both want it. It's not because I'm taking your firsts or you're giving them. They're not some property to be bartered away. This is all for pleasure."

My nails dig a trail down the back of his neck, digging in slightly until he's grinning at me again.

"Pleasure and maybe a little bit of pain," I growl.

He growls back, nipping at my earlobe as wetness pools between my legs. I'm dripping with need for him—and love, but I won't admit the love part out loud. The things he's done to protect me are very loving; I admit it. I can't deny that what he feels for me is true, even if it's not the only reason for his actions.

Do I love him?

It doesn't matter. All I know is I want to taste his cock, I want him to lick every part of me, and I want him to drive his cock inside me. I want him to take my virginity and any other first these sick men think they are salivating over. I don't care if I have to give all the money back. I realize now that letting them get any of my firsts is not worth getting my revenge. I can find another way.

His hand splays across my belly before pausing at the top of my panties.

"How wet are you? I can't wait to find out," he says.

My breath catches in my throat as his fingers lift my panties from my body and slide under the fabric. I freeze as his fingers travel down across the flesh of my lower stomach until he reaches...

I gasp as his finger slides across my slit, feeling how soaked I am. He can feel how desperately I need him.

"So wet, so hungry. Tell me, Lilith, will you stab me if I don't make you come?" he grins against my neck as he says it.

I, on the other hand, can barely remind my body to breathe, let alone speak, as his fingers move over my sensitive bundle of nerves. God, it feels beyond what pleasure should feel like. It feels too good—I'm going to be addicted to his touch. I don't know how I'll ever get anything else done when this is all I'll ever want to do.

"I think you would." His thumb sweeps across me, and the sound that leaves my body is pure bliss mixed with the agony of needing more of him and not knowing how he's going to satisfy me more. "Good thing I want to make you come more than I want anything else on this earth."

The second the words leave his lips, he growls, and my panties are ripped from my body. His lips land on mine in a devouring kiss that leaves me breathless. My legs wrap around his body, and I'm cursing that he's still wearing his pants and my shirt is still on. I want every part of him touching every part of me. I want to feel everything. I want and want and want.

"Don't worry, Lilith, I've got you," Hayes says as if he can read my mind.

I don't know what that means, but a second later, he's vanished from my arms, sitting back on his heels between my legs. My shirt is scrunched up under my arms, revealing my entire body to him.

His appreciative gaze burns through my skin, my darkest secrets, and the desire I've only ever felt for him on full display. And then his gaze narrows in on my pussy spread wide for him.

He licks his lips in anticipation, like he's about to eat the most delicious cake instead of tasting me.

I squirm slightly, waiting for him to do what the glimmer in his eyes promises. I don't know how I feel about having his lips there. I've never wanted a man to taste me, to fuck me, to stretch me, and make me come. But then, I've never met a man like Hayes before.

I move my thighs slightly together.

"Don't you dare," he growls, spreading me as wide as I can go again.

I bite my lip. "Fuck me, Hayes. Take my virginity. Take it all."

A darkness clouds his eyes, and that grin curls higher into a wicked grin across his entire face.

"Let's see how loud I can make you scream, Lilith."

And then his face lowers to between my thighs, and his tongue sweeps up my slit and across my clit. The sensations shooting through me are so intense and overwhelming that my legs tighten around his head.

Hayes chuckles, which shoots unyielding pleasure up and down my body. His hands gently spread my thighs again so he can breathe.

My hands find the bun on top of his head, and my fingers sink into his hair as his tongue lashes against my sensitive bud.

He's relentless with his tongue—sweeping over me again and again. More wetness spills out of me, and I know he can taste it.

"Sweet and tart, just like you," he says.

I open my mouth to speak, but then I feel one of his fingers pressing at my entrance. I can't do anything but focus on his strong fingers sliding through my slickness and inside me.

"Oh, that feels...fuck..." I moan.

He grins as his tongue continues to swirl across my clit, and his fingers push in and out of me in long, stroking motions.

His two fingers are half the width of his cock and nowhere near as long. When he fucks me, he'll spread me so wide I won't be able to breathe. And yet, it's all I want.

I want him—all of him.

A shudder starts, and my body seizes as I lose control. My toes curl, my back arches, and my thighs clench around his head again.

What's happening?

What's—?

I explode.

I've touched myself numerous times. I love a good vibrator, but I've never felt anything like this.

Stars spark behind my eyes as his tongue and fingers continue to work my body until they've milked every last drop of my orgasm from me. He continues until I'm so sensitive I can feel every hair of his gruff five o'clock shadow against my thighs, every nerve ending in my body, and every whisper of his breath against my core.

I sink into the bed as my eyes drift closed for only a second. We aren't done; that was only round one. I need all of the rounds. I need everything now—I can't wait.

His body leaves mine, and my eyes flash open to see him walking toward the door.

"Where are you going?" I say with annoyance in my voice.

Hayes pauses and looks at me with longing in his eyes. "Sleep, Lily. Tomorrow we need to train and make a plan to get your revenge."

He's out the door before I can get a single syllable out. I run to the door and glance down the hallway to see him disappear into the room next to mine.

"Hayes!" I shout at him as I race to his door. The door slams shut, and I can hear the lock turning, but I try it anyway.

It doesn't budge. I can pick locks, and this one seems easy enough, but I won't push him. It's clear he doesn't want more from me or won't let himself take more.

I didn't even get to taste him, to lick him, to bring him pleasure. A theory goes through my head at that, but I don't dare speak it or let myself think on it for long. It means Hayes is more broken than I realized. His smile and constant laughter form a facade—a protective mechanism.

I rest my hand on the door, knowing how I'll spend tomorrow. Instead of planning my revenge with him, I'll be finding a way to give him the pleasure he just gave me.

A soft smile spreads across my face at the wave of bliss he gave me and all the joy he has yet to give me. He's right to take our time and experience everything. It makes every moment more special. After all, we are to be married in a couple of weeks, and then we will have a lifetime to spend fucking each other senseless.

CHAPTER 20

Lilith

I WAKE up grinning like a fool. A fool that let the first man who ever gave me an orgasm change all of my plans. A fool dancing with a happiness I haven't felt in a very long time.

I skip to the kitchen, hoping to find Hayes. All night I dreamt of his kisses, of his hot tongue against my body, and the pleasure I could pull from him when I finally get my turn. My fluttering heart drops when I don't see his overly happy face grinning back at me. I'm not going to get that good morning kiss.

Where is he?

I walk further into the kitchen, spotting a plate of food and a cup of coffee in front of one of the bar stools. A folded note is tucked under the coffee cup with my name written in beautiful cursive.

I pick up the note and read.

Eat up, you're going to need your strength for what I have planned for you today. When you're finished, get dressed, and meet me in the basement.

My smile extends so far across my face that my jaw begins to hurt. I can only imagine what dirty things Hayes has in mind, so I start shoveling in food as fast as I can.

The food is still warm, so he must have finished making this recently. Eggs Benedict—fucking delicious. It's a shame he went through all this effort to make a beautiful breakfast for me, and I'm not savoring it. But there will be time to savor his meals in the future. Right now, I need to find him.

I change into the first clothes I find—a sports bra and leggings. I don't even bother with a shirt, knowing he'd rip it from my body. My hair is a rat's nest of tangled red curls, but his hands will be running through it soon enough.

Running down the stairs to the basement, my heart thunders in my chest. It slams to a stop when I see what's in the basement.

Hayes is shirtless—his sculpted muscles glistening with sweat as he faces a shirtless Gage in a sparring ring. He didn't request me to come down here to fuck me senseless. I'm here to train.

It's back to business this morning.

Hayes throws a punch, knocking Gage to the ground. Gage offers him a rare smile as Hayes holds out his hand to him to help him to stand. Then both of their heads snap in my direction.

A flash of heat swirls in Hayes's eyes when he sees me, but it's gone as quickly as it appeared. Gage continues to look at me with suspicion, as if I'm their enemy, not the rest of the Retribution Kings. Gage doesn't trust me, but the feeling is mutual.

Heat dampens in my core, even though I should focus on getting them to talk, to trust me, and to help me get revenge. But it's hard when Hayes looks like that—all hard muscle, a hot tattoo, long hair I want to run my hands through, and those dark full-framed glasses that brighten his eyes. And don't get me started on what I know his shorts are hiding.

"We're working on your training today," Hayes says.

"I don't need training. I know enough." I fold my arms, my grumpy demeanor instantly returning.

Hayes grins, his sunshiny self reappearing.

I sigh. Things are back to how they were before.

"Prove it. Disarm Gage."

I glance at Gage, not wanting to get near the guy. Hayes is large, but Gage is bigger by at least a couple of inches. He has thicker muscles, and his constant serious glare is scary enough to keep me at bay.

Gage walks over to his bag and pulls out a gun. He makes a show of emptying it to prove it's not loaded.

I frown.

"What weapon do I get?"

"Nothing," Gage says. "Prove you can disarm me before I shoot you dead, and you'll have no need for training."

"If I do it, will you both trust me enough to tell me your plan?"

Hayes raises his eyebrows at Gage. *Maybe it's Gage I need to win over, not Hayes? Hayes might tell me everything if Gage allowed it.*

Gage's eyes never leave mine. "Yes."

My eyes widen. I wasn't expecting it to be that easy.

"Rules?" I ask.

"There are none," Gage says.

Well, okay then.

I walk onto the mat Hayes and Gage were sparring on,

while Hayes walks off the edge. He leans against the wall, not bothering to sit down. He thinks this fight will be short. *But who is he betting on? Me or Gage?*

Adrenaline beats through my body, and I take a deep calming breath as I face Gage. He's holding the gun casually to one side, not even bothering to aim it at me.

It's a trap. I know it. But if I can beat Gage, I can prove to him I'm worth trusting.

"Are you going to try to disarm me, or are you just going to stand there and be an easy target?" Gage goads me.

I grind my teeth together, and then I run at Gage full speed. He raises the gun at me, and I slide out like I'm sliding into home base on a baseball field.

I take Gage down before he gets a good aim at me. My hand knocks the gun from his hand as he lands hard on top of me. God, he weighs a ton. Hayes would try to cushion his fall on top of me, but Gage offers no such nicety. I'm going to be bruised from the impact. But I did it, so it will be worth it.

I grin widely, knowing I won. I hope it's enough to gain Gage's trust.

"Bam, you're dead," Gage says.

I frown as I feel the barrel of a gun pressed against my temple.

My eyes cut to the side, where I see the gun I knocked out of his hands lying on the floor. This is a new gun.

"That's not fair. I disarmed you!"

Gage shakes his head. "You didn't. You knocked one gun out of my hand. You didn't disarm me. You didn't ensure I only had one weapon on me. You assumed I only had one when you saw me get one gun from the bag. You got cocky and failed just like I knew you would."

"That's cheating," I complain.

"There is no such thing, not in this world." Gage gets off

of me, his expression somehow more serious than ever. He doesn't offer his hand to help me up. He just towers over me, making me feel small.

I frown.

Hayes walks over and offers his hand to me, but I don't accept it. I stand up on my own.

"Fine, I'll train."

———

Eight hours later, I'm ready for bed. And not with Hayes, just to sleep. They've kept me training for eight hours. I don't know how I'm still standing in this basement.

Their reasoning is we don't have time. We need to take advantage of every second we have. I don't know why they think we have so little time to train. The only thing I can think of is the wedding. I've been given very few details of what will happen at the wedding or who will show up. My guess is that our wedding will be flooded with Retribution Kings, and maybe they have a plan to use the wedding as a way to get our revenge.

Despite all the training, they haven't shared a whisper of their plan with me.

"What did the Retribution Kings do to you? To you both? Why do you hate them?" I ask.

Gage exchanges a silent look with Hayes. Gage wipes the sweat from his brow, grabs his bag, and then leaves without a word or look in my direction.

I sigh. "He's never going to trust me, is he?"

Hayes glances at the stairs Gage just disappeared up. "Give him time."

"What about you? Do you trust me enough to share your truth with me?"

Hayes takes a deep breath but doesn't say anything.

"My father was killed by the Retribution Kings, but I'm sure you know that. Everyone does. What everyone doesn't know is why. The lie is that he betrayed the Retribution Kings. He was planning to destroy them. He wanted power and money. He was working for a rival gang. He was a spy. But none of that is true," I say.

Tears well in my eyes as I think about my father. "His only mistake was not killing a man. He was sent on a mission to kill a man who had stolen from the Retribution Kings. But he couldn't do it when he realized the man had two young sons and had stolen to feed his family. My father paid the price instead."

Hayes stares at me with his piercing green eyes. He doesn't say anything. He doesn't tell me he's sorry. He doesn't offer me any condolences.

Slowly, he walks toward me and tucks a strand of hair behind my ear before grazing a soft kiss on my forehead.

"Come. I'll make you something to eat."

He doesn't open up. He doesn't offer me any of his own history. And he doesn't offer any of his thoughts about what happened to my father. He shuts me out.

My heart aches, desperate to learn more, to find the flirty, fun-loving guy again. But deep down, he's as broken as I am.

Let me in, and I'll help you rebuild the pieces.

He doesn't—at least, not today.

He will. He just needs time.

As my heart aches for him, I wonder a realization—*who really loves who?*

CHAPTER 21

Hayes

LILITH STANDS from the bar stool after finishing every bite of her chicken parmesan.

"I'm going to bed," she says.

I grab her hand, stopping her mid-step. She doesn't bother to turn and look at me, but that doesn't stop her from telling me off.

"I'm exhausted. You both proved your point that I'm not in shape or ready to fight the Retribution Kings on my own. But I will be. So unless you're ready to trust me with your secrets, let me sleep and try again tomorrow."

I trust her; that's not the problem. And she's more than ready to face the Retribution Kings. Today wasn't about making her prove herself. It was about distracting us after I got a phone call from Peter, followed by one from Titus. I know what's expected of me—of us.

"I know," I say, my eyes darkening and my grin returning. I will do everything in my power to make this enjoyable for her. To take away all of her fear. To protect her at all costs. Even if it means pretending I'm happy and calm when I'm the furthest thing from it.

Turning to me, she yawns as if trying to prove her point. "Then what do you want?"

"Let me help you sleep."

She frowns and tilts her head in confusion. She'd fall asleep the second her head hits the pillow as it is. Still, I pull her to me in one hard yank of her hand. She falls into my chest, her breathing hard and ragged.

I lift my thumb to her lip and brush over it. She shivers at my touch, her cheeks pinking. And then her eyes lock on mine, and need flashes across her face.

"We can't delay the next first any longer."

She stills as she realizes what I could only protect her from for so long and pretend I could find a way out of. But both Peter and Titus made it clear that I can't back out of this. The consequences will be severe if I do.

I grin widely, a smolder on my face that hints at all the devious and delicious things I want to do to her body, trying to calm her nerves. Fear still flickers in her eyes.

Leaning down, I kiss her. It's a desperate kiss, where I don't hold back. I kiss her with everything I have, forcing my mind to think of only her. My worry disappears the second my lips land on hers. Our bodies press together, fitting together like we're cut from the same puzzle.

When my lips release hers, we're both panting. We're so desperate to feel each other that filming our intimate moment and knowing other disgusting men are watching no longer matters. All that matters is us.

"What first is this?" she asks, her breath hot against my lip.

"Worshipping your body until you come."

"Something you've already given me."

I shake my head, sucking her bottom lip again tenderly. "Something I haven't done nearly enough."

"I won't have to pretend it's our first time. Every time

you kiss me, it feels like the first time. It's like this is all a dream when I'm with you." Her hooded eyes meet mine. "Is it always like this? Or is this feeling because it's us?"

God, I'm fucking hard for her. It's going to take everything in me not to fuck her senseless. But I want her to know the truth—as much of it as I can share with her—before I fuck her. I want her to actually choose me when I bury myself deep inside her. Because once I do, I won't be able to stop fucking her.

"I can't speak for you. Maybe you'd feel this way with another man. But for me, it's never like this. I've only ever felt this way with you."

Desire flashes in her eyes. "I can't imagine feeling this way with anyone but you."

And then our lips find each other again—hard and punishing. The impact rolls through us quickly, the need escalating into uncontrollable fervor.

My hands slide up her leggings, and I lift her under her thighs. She wraps her legs around my waist and throws her hands around my neck.

Our lips never leave each other as I lift her onto the bar. Our hands tangle into each other's hair. I tilt her head back, giving me access to kiss down the delicate skin of her neck.

Moans escape her throat with each peppered kiss. Her fingers dig into my scalp as she yanks my lips back to her mouth, where I catch her next whimpers against my lips.

My cock hardens between her legs, and I push against her, letting her feel the effect she has on my body. Her legs wrap around me like a vice grip.

I growl at her possessiveness. The only good thing about the deal I made is that it will be clear to everyone that Lilith is mine—fucking mine.

But she's not.

I push that voice out. *She will be. She has to be. I won't let her go. I won't let the Retribution Kings have her.*

"Take me to bed," Lilith says, her voice sultry and sweet. I know she's doing it for my benefit. She's giving me permission to take her to the bed where the Retribution Kings are waiting for us.

"No, I want you right here." I lean in and capture her lips with mine as my hands slide down the curves of her body.

She arches into me, unable to stop her body from reacting to my touch. Her nails slide down my back, no doubt drawing blood and leaving a mark I will wear with honor as she claims me as hers.

Suddenly, she shoves me hard.

"Take. Me. To. Bed," she growls.

My shoulders slump. *I'm not sure I can do this.*

Her hand softly strokes my cheek, and she nods.

She wants this.

I want this.

Who cares that others are watching?

You don't ever want to take from her again. You've hurt her enough already.

I shake off those thoughts and flash her a seductive grin as I turn on the Hayes that she and the rest of the world are familiar with.

She bites her bottom lip.

I sweep her off the counter, wrapping her legs tight around my waist once again as I carry her to the bedroom.

I nip at her earlobe.

"I've been thinking about tasting you again all day. I want to see if you taste as sweet as I remember. If the little whimpers you made when you came were real. If you falling apart will make my world spin again."

"Hurry," she whispers.

I grin genuinely.

We make it to the door of the bedroom, and I don't hesitate. I need to be strong for her once she realizes what's going on.

A dozen men are standing around the bed. Apparently, testing her in person is more important than making sure none of them end up dead again. There is no way to avoid them seeing us, seeing Lilith.

My throat dries at the thought of them watching her, of them being so close to her. It's not because I don't think it's hot as hell to fuck her while others watch. But I know who these men are, and what they will request of her, what they will do to her. I know the monsters they are.

And as much as we both might want to kill them all, we'd fail. Peter has a security team on standby outside the house. We'd have to take out dozens and dozens of men and still wouldn't kill enough of the leaders in the Retribution Kings to make a difference when it comes to getting revenge for Lilith. We would die, and it would all be for nothing.

Lilith kisses me hot and heavy, not holding back, dragging my mind and body back to her and away from the dark abyss. My mind is barely even acknowledging that there are men in the room with us, watching us, ready to pounce if we make a wrong move. She knew what awaited us, even if I didn't speak the words out loud.

We fall onto the bed, with me on top of her. I try to shield her for as long as I can, but they are fucking everywhere. There is no hiding this time.

My arms tremble slightly, and my eyes widen, begging her to find a way out of this. For her to plead with me to let her go. If she said she couldn't do this, then I'd find a way for her to escape. I'd do anything to protect her from this.

Instead of whispers begging me to help her, I see lust-filled eyes as she drags her tongue across her bottom lip.

"Make me come, Hayes. Let's put on a show for these bastards." Her seductive, vengeful grin is almost my undoing.

I growl, knowing we're in this deep. Despite the sick bastards staring at us, I'm going to make sure she enjoys every fucking second of this. We both grin one last time before I devour her.

"Strip her bare," Peter says as if giving instructions on how to build a piece of furniture.

I flip my head in his direction as a menacing growl leaves my lips.

He doesn't look the least bit surprised or annoyed by my reaction. His face remains as blank and bored as ever.

"I can handle this without you barking orders at me every second."

"True, but she needs to be tested. It's even more vital now," he replies.

I frown, not sure what has changed that makes testing her more important. But I know hesitating and arguing every point is moot. I'll have to strip her. I'll have to do a lot of things to her in front of them. I can't fight the easy orders.

I turn my gaze back to Lilith and flash her my signature smile. Her eyes smile back with a sultry fire in them.

"Keep your eyes on me," I say, before I lower my lips to hers.

Our tongues tangle, and our eyes stay open and on each other. I don't want her closing her eyes and imagining what's going on in the darkness. I want her looking at me.

My hand rests on her hip as I slowly trail up her bare skin to the sports bra she's wearing. Her tongue lashes against mine, and I slip my hand under her bra, pushing it up over her swollen breasts and head. Pebbled nipples meet my fingers as I brush my thumb across the tip of one and then the other.

She gasps into my mouth as heat floods her core. Her hips roll to meet mine, and I feel myself harden even more beneath my pants. I don't know how I'm only supposed to make her come, but I'll have to behave until they all leave.

That is, if she even still wants me when this is over...

I lock onto that feeling of arousal, forcing the truth of what I'm doing out of my mind. My hands skim over her waist, hooking my fingers into her yoga pants and sliding them down and off her ankles until she's bare in front of me.

I don't hesitate, knowing the longer I stare at her glorious body, the better view I'm giving the others. And if I give them a moment to think, they'll bark orders at me of vile things they want me to do to her.

My tongue sweeps around her soaked slit, tasting all the sweetness I've already spilled from her body with every kiss. Lilith's eyes are honed into mine. I know I'm all she sees.

I'm going to make this quick. I'll have her coming before the others even realize what's happening. And then I'll have reason to kick them all out when I've taken her first orgasm.

But they'll be back. Round after round, milking this until the wedding day.

I push those disturbing thoughts out of my mind as her hands sink into my hair, pulling it loose from the bun. My glasses fall down my nose, making her chuckle softly.

The chuckle quickly turns into soft whimpers, edging closer to moans, and then my name hovers on her lips as I feel her getting close.

I slip a finger through her wetness, inching her closer to that bliss that will soon swallow her whole.

You're so close, murderous one. So close. Come, and this can all be over. Come, and I'll fuck you for real—over and over again in my bed until you're so sore you can't think straight. Come, release your orgasm. Don't hold anything back, and this can end.

Her fingers dig deeper into my scalp, and her thighs tighten around my face, squeezing hard as she pants quickly. She's seconds away—

"Stop," Peter yells.

Stop? What?

I can't stop. She's so—

My head is yanked back, and my arms are pulled behind my back by two men. I'm forced to sit on the edge of the bed on my knees. I watch in horror as two men grab Lilith's arms, holding her to the bed.

I try to shake the men off, until I see the gun aimed at Lilith's head. I still immediately.

"What the hell is going on? I was supposed to taste her and give her an orgasm. That's what I was doing. What the fuck is this?" I bark out; my anger is palpable, and my body is tense.

"This is a test, for both of you. You've grown fond of Lilith, boy, but she hasn't gained our trust, not yet. Two of our men ended up dead, most likely because of her."

I freeze. *Have they figured out that Lilith is a killer? That between the two of us, we could fight our way out of this room?* We'd still end up dead, but right now, it feels worth it.

"Retribution Kings are all about loyalty and following commands, even if the commands don't make sense. There is a hierarchy. Lilith has to be tested. And for that matter, you should still be tested as well."

They want me to hurt her to see if she'll save herself or if someone will come to her rescue. Neither of those things will happen. She won't save herself. And there is no one coming. I'm the only one who can protect her.

"Did Titus agree to this?" I ask, knowing his word matters above all else. If he didn't agree, then everyone in this room will be dead when he hears about it.

"It was his idea," Peter answers.

"Bullshit. He would never agree to this when…" I don't finish my sentence. It's too painful.

Lilith cocks an eyebrow, clearly confused as to what I was about to say, confused about all of this.

I'm sorry, I say to her in my mind. It's not enough. It was one thing to bring her pleasure in front of them. Whatever this is, it's not going to be of either of our choosing.

A subtle nod is her response. She's still with me. And as soon as we survive this, I'll tell her everything. No more secrets. I don't care what Gage or Lennox or Titus or anyone else says.

"Titus will kill you all for this," I growl.

"As I said, it was his idea. You both need to be tested," Peter says, sounding bored.

"What is the test?" Lilith asks.

Peter finally looks at her, as if remembering she's a human with her own choice in all of this. But he doesn't answer her.

She huffs and looks at me. "Do it. Whatever they want, do it."

So strong, so brave, my murderous one. My Lily.

My eyes grow as determined as hers.

I nod.

To my surprise, I'm shoved back between her still-spread legs. My arms are still held behind my back. Lilith is still held down on the bed by two men's hands.

"Lick her, bring her to the edge of an orgasm," Peter says.

I hesitate, confused by his request, but I do as he says. My tongue flicks over her clit, and her wetness spills from her in spades. Her stomach rises and falls quickly, her teeth raking over her bottom lip. Despite everything, she's still turned on, still so ready for me.

I growl over her clit before my tongue slips inside of her,

pulling her wetness out before I pull out to massage her sensitive bud again. In and out, I keep the pattern up until I can see the orgasm starting.

"Hay—" she starts to cry out, and then suddenly, I'm jerked away from her.

Her cry stops and turns into a whimper of need. She needs me to help her finish.

"That was cruel," she says, whipping her head to Peter.

His lips thin. "You haven't seen cruel yet. Again."

I'm shoved down onto the space between her legs harder this time. My tongue immediately goes to work on her body. I try to build her slower this time, so it's not so painful when her orgasm doesn't happen. But she's so turned on that one brush of my tongue against her has her edging.

I'm ripped from her body again.

She squirms on the bed, but the two men continue to hold her down forcefully, not letting her move an inch.

Stay with me. But she slams her eyes closed, unable to keep her gaze on me.

"Again," Peter says.

Fuck.

Again, I'm thrown between her legs. I change tactics, swirling my tongue over her quickly, hoping she'll come before they realize what's happening. But they catch on to what I'm doing, and I'm ripped away.

Over.

And over.

And over.

Tears begin down her cheeks in a single streak. It's the only sign of the pain she's in, the frustration that will never end. *How much longer can she endure? How is this going to end?*

I grind my teeth together—with me. It ends with me.

Her tears undo me.

I'm lowered, but this time I break free and grip onto her thighs. I nip at her clit, knowing the intensity will be enough to undo her.

"Hayes!" she screams, arching into me.

I hold onto her as long as I can, until I've milked all of her orgasm from her body, and I feel her body relax beneath me—the tears slowing.

When I'm pulled back, I twist out of the hold again. I throw a punch and sweep for the gun on the waist of one of my enforcers.

When I aim the gun, it's at Peter.

His eyes flash wide for a single second, before regaining his composure.

"Get Gage in here," I say. He's the only one I trust.

"You disappoint me, Hayes."

"I don't care what you think of me, Peter. If you don't want to die, get Gage in here, *now*."

Peter nods to one of his men.

A few seconds later, Gage walks in. He quickly assesses the situation with a dark glare.

"Lilith leaves with Gage, and I'll let you live."

Peter nods to Gage. Gage walks over to the bed, and Lilith is released. He scoops her up effortlessly in his arms, cradling her so her naked body is as protected as it can be. Then he carries her out of the room.

"No, wait, what about Hayes?" Lilith asks in a panicked voice.

"I've got you. Let Hayes worry about Hayes," I hear Gage say, nearly out of the room.

Lilith doesn't accept that. She tries to break free of Gage's arms, and she almost gets free.

"I'm right behind you. Trust me," I say, looking at her with a calmness I only feel when I'm with her.

She accepts my words, and then Gage carries her out

even though he knows my words are a lie. There is no way I'm walking out of here after her. Gage is only allowed to carry her out because of Titus.

Titus is the only one that can save either of us now, and I'm still not sure I can trust him.

The second she's gone, I lower my gun, knowing I've lost. But Lilith's safe.

"That was foolish, boy. And now you'll pay—for everything," Peter says.

CHAPTER 22

Lilith

"YOU SHOULD TRY TO SLEEP," Gage says from the corner chair of my bedroom.

Over and over I pace back and forth, unable to clear my mind or rid myself of the nervous energy thumping through my veins.

"I can't."

Gage doesn't tell me to sleep again, but his eyes watch me pace. His gaze cuts down to his phone screen every few seconds.

"What are you looking at?"

"Security camera feeds. I have eyes on all of the Retribution Kings."

I raise my eyebrows as I continue to walk. "Any sign of Hayes?"

Gage swallows hard. "Hayes will be fine."

"How do you know that? He betrayed them. They'll kill him for it."

Gage shakes his head. "Hayes is far too valuable for them to ever kill. Titus made him his number two for a reason. He'll be punished for his disobedience, but that's it."

"That's it?" I stop, shooting daggers from my eyes toward Gage. "Being punished doesn't mean he'll survive."

"Hayes always survives. He'll be fine. And so will you. But you'll be more useful to Hayes if you sleep."

I scoff and continue pacing. Burying my nose in Haye's T-shirt I'm still wearing, I take a deep breath to inhale his scent.

"I still can't believe Hayes did that. He didn't need to protect me. It wasn't that bad. I wasn't really in any pain. It was torture, yes, but nothing I couldn't endure. He should have known..."

"Should have known what?"

I pause, my eyes snapping to Gage. "That Hayes being punished on my behalf would be far worse for me to endure than any physical torture."

"You love him?"

My heart flutters to a stop. I shrug. "I promised to never love someone I could lose again."

Gage nods. "Wise, and yet it appears you've broken your promise."

I stare at the floor as my legs tremble, resuming my pacing. I can't keep this up much longer. I've been pacing for hours. I should sit, but I can't—not when Hayes is enduring god knows what.

"What about reading or watching TV in bed? Or soaking in the tub if you won't sleep? Hayes will tell you everything when he returns—the plan for revenge, the..."

"I don't care about any revenge plan unless it includes revenge for Hayes." I stop, shocked by my own words. It's the truth. Right now, imagining all the horrible pain Hayes could be in—all I want is revenge for Hayes. Everything else can wait.

Gage narrows his eyes at me and nods.

I walk over to him, not sure what I'm doing. Gage grabs

my hand and pulls me into his lap, wrapping his arms around me in a hug.

I shatter in his arms—tears falling freely and my body shaking with fear.

"He'll be okay. He'll survive this. And you'll get a chance to tell him how you feel."

The tears fall harder and uncontrollably. I feel his hand running up and down my back, trying to comfort me, even though I know this isn't who Gage is. He's not the one people seek out for comfort. He's the one people seek out for information. He knows Hayes's location, and what's happening to him, I know it.

I wipe my tears on the shoulder of his shirt.

"Tell me where he is."

"You can't go to him. You can't save him. And he would kill me if I let you try."

I shake my head. "He deserves to be saved. He would do it if it were me."

"Yes, he does."

"But you still won't tell me?" I grit out.

"No, I won't. He doesn't need saving from this. He'll need help when it's over, but there's nothing to do now."

I frown, pushing off Gage's chest and glaring at him. "Tell me what they're doing to him. Tell me what torture he's enduring. If you expect me to be able to help him when he returns, then help me prepare for the trauma he's experiencing."

Gage's tight eyes cut through mine, as if he's still assessing where my loyalties lie. Finally, he speaks. "You already know."

My heart squeezes in my chest as I put the pieces together. My stomach drops, and I can barely breathe at the thought.

"I think I'm going to be sick."

Gage resumes rubbing my back. "Do it now, before he returns."

He doesn't say it, but it's clear Gage expects me to be strong when Hayes returns. That's why he wants me to sleep or at least rest. But my mind is spinning with what is most likely happening to Hayes.

Red—all I see is hot, red rage. *They are all going to pay for this.*

Gage squeezes me, and I rest my head on his shoulder again. I curl up in his lap, closing my eyes and plotting my revenge.

"Lilith," Gage's voice sounds in my head in a whisper.

I open my eyes, confused about how I could have fallen asleep on Gage's lap. I don't know how long I was out, and Gage is still holding me.

I sit up, and he shows me his phone. "Hayes is back."

Hayes is walking up the stairs of the house, alone. He looks tired and exhausted, but he's alive.

I jump off Gage's lap, running my hand through my hair and trying to think of what to say or do.

Gage stands, watching me closely, his eyes cutting to the phone every few seconds.

I start pacing again, but Gage grabs me. "No, he needs you now."

I stop and nod. He's right. He's saved me countless times; I'll do anything to help him.

Gage's eyes cut to the door behind me, and he whispers in my ear, "Forgive him."

I cock an eyebrow, not having a clue why I would need to forgive Hayes. There is nothing he could do that would warrant my forgiveness. He survived—that's all he needed to do.

Gage releases me and walks to the door, where I know Hayes has entered, but I haven't turned to face him yet.

"I'll make sure you're both safe," Gage says. I hear him pat Hayes on the shoulder, and then his heavy feet walk out of the room.

Slowly, I turn to face Hayes.

Hayes grins at me, his dimple deep on his cheek, and his eyes bright with amusement.

It's an act—for me. He's protecting me from the pain or trauma he experienced. Saving him from himself won't be easy. He'll have to let me in and stop pretending he's okay when he isn't.

I'm ready for the challenge.

I run to him, throwing my arms around him. He catches me in his arms, and we plant our lips on each other in a deep kiss.

When he comes up for air, he takes a deep breath, his body relaxing in my arms. "I'm okay. I'm not hurt, Lily. Are you okay? I'm so sorry. Let me look at you."

He tilts my head up to look me in the eye. He needs to see that I'm okay, when I should be the one doing that to him.

"I'm fine, thanks to you."

He nods, his smile glued to his face like a shield.

What happened to you, Hayes? What agony did you endure?

I don't ask that out loud. It's too soon. And the question could hurt more than help.

I wrap my arms around him tightly, noticing that he flinches slightly as I do. But I don't see any physical sign of injury. It's like he can't be touched but wants to be touched at the same time.

I force myself to let go until I figure out how to help him. I take a deep breath—expecting to smell his familiar musky, masculine scent. Instead, I get a whiff of sweet perfume and sweat.

I swallow hard, realizing what he smells like. He smells like sex. And it's not my scent that's all over him. My eyes water, but I don't let the tears fall.

Oh, my Hayes, what did they make you do?

Forgive him, Gage's words return to me.

I grind my teeth together. There is nothing to forgive. I only see murder.

Hayes realizes the moment I realize what happened. He strokes my cheek. "It's okay, murderous one, we'll get revenge."

"We will. We'll kill them all for what they did to you," I reply.

CHAPTER 23

Hayes

HER STARE IS SATURATED with pain and revenge, realizing the truth of what happened without me having to speak a word. She knows me better than I thought if she figured it out so quickly. Gage wouldn't have told her what I endured. It's a torture I'd suffer over and over and over again if it meant protecting her.

Unfortunately, I still haven't figured out how to protect her from the rest of it. The Retribution Kings trust her more now than before, but trust isn't enough.

She takes my hand in hers and squeezes it with a soft smile. I expect to see hurt in her eyes—for her to be angry with me for what I did. I should have to beg on my knees for forgiveness. I betrayed her even when I didn't want to.

"Don't," she says before I even open my mouth. "Don't you dare apologize. You didn't hurt me. You survived. You're alive. You have nothing to apologize for."

I reach out, tucking a strand of her red hair behind her ear. "I don't deserve you."

She bats her eyelashes at me, a wicked grin spreading over her face. "Can I wash you?"

My eyebrows shoot up; I wasn't expecting that. Even more shocking, her look says she has dirty ideas in mind.

I take a deep breath, not sure exactly what I want or need or can even tolerate. Her touch is enough and yet not enough.

She senses my hesitation.

"We don't have to do anything other than wash. I just thought you'd feel better after a shower. Then sleep might help. If you want more or less... I'll give you whatever you need. I just don't want you to be alone right now, even if you don't want to be touched."

"A shower would be good," I reply.

She gives me a tight smile and guides me to the bathroom. Her hand never lets go of mine, and she doesn't force any other touch.

She walks to the shower, turns it on, and then stops. Her voice comes out soft and wispy. "Do you want me to give you privacy?"

"No, stay. Shower with me."

She exhales a long breath of relief.

I do as well.

Then she grabs the hem of the T-shirt she's wearing, one of my T-shirts, and lifts it over her head in one swoop. She stands before me in nothing but black panties, and I suck in a breath at the sight of her.

After the night I had, I'd forgotten how breathtakingly beautiful she is. Her every curve and freckle brings me back to life and makes me want to lick and taste every spot on her.

But images of what happened tonight flash in my head, and I squeeze my eyes shut. I feel her fingers brush against mine, and I shiver.

"Keep your eyes on me," she says gently, repeating the words I told her earlier tonight.

I open my eyes and stare at her, forcing my familiar grin.

"You're right. Why close my eyes when I have such a beautiful woman standing in front of me."

She smiles. "You don't have to make jokes if you don't want to. You don't have to do anything you don't want to, not now. And never again if I have any say in it."

"Jokes and laughter are all I know."

I wait for her to offer to help me strip or to get a washcloth to rid me of the scent of another woman. Instead, I cock my head in confusion when she reaches into the shower. She grabs the handheld, and she sprays me, fully clothed.

My mouth gapes, and a wicked grin grows on my cheeks.

"You did not just do that," I say.

She laughs. "What are you going to do about it, sunshine?"

"This." I grab her by the hips as she continues to spray me over and over with the shower head. I shove her back under the spray of the rain shower, grabbing the handheld out of her grip.

I spin her around, until her ass is against my crotch, and then I direct the spray between her legs.

She gasps, "Not fair."

I chuckle as I nip at her ear and breathe her in. She reaches back, loosening my soaked bun until she frees my hair.

My free hand palms her breast as the other continues to torture her clit with the water. She quickly falls apart, her moans ricocheting off the bathroom tiles.

"You're fucking amazing," I say against her ear.

"And you're about to get payback for that." She turns, knocking the sprayer out of my hand and reaching for the button of my jeans. She undoes it quickly, unzips the jeans, and peels the wet cloth down my thighs until my pierced cock springs free.

I'm not sure what she's going to do, and flashes of images in my head remind me why I shouldn't do this. My heart thunders in my chest at the thought of being touched so soon after...

She kneels in front of me, water dripping down her face. Her green eyes peer up at me, and my mind clears, except for her.

"Can I?" she asks. She doesn't take; she waits for me.

I nod, knowing I need this.

We both do.

Her tongue dips out of her mouth, and she carefully licks over my tip gently, like a caress.

I gasp, my eyes watching her closely, and hers mine for any reaction. She'll stop if it becomes too much before I even get the word out. But I'll never ask her to stop.

Another lick, this one starting at my base and up my length. I still, terrified I'll shatter and break under her touch.

But when she wraps her lips around me, sucking me deep in her mouth in one swallow...

I'm hers—fucking hers.

She claims all of me with her mouth as she slides up and down the length of me. Her tongue finds my piercing and flicks over it. Ecstasy rushes through me.

I reach my hand down, trying to find a way to pleasure her as she does this. She can't be comfortable on her knees like that, gagging on my cock...

She pushes my hand away. "Please, let me."

Her words couldn't be any clearer. This moment is about my pleasure, not hers.

I nod, even though it kills me. But as her mouth pulls me in and out, I'm lost to only thinking about how fucking good this feels. I don't feel anything else. No other memories pop into my head.

I've gotten countless blow jobs before, but none that ever felt like this.

My hand sinks into her hair. "I'm going to—"

She grins around me, and I explode down her throat.

"Lily!" I cry out as warm cum shoots into her.

She holds me in her mouth until the orgasm ripples through me completely. Then she stands, the biggest smile on her lips. But it's not bigger than the smile on mine.

She grabs the hem of my wet shirt and peels it off, tossing it in a puddle on the shower floor.

Grabbing a bottle of body wash from behind me, she squirts some on me and then herself. Neither of us scrubs our bodies. We let the water run the soap over us and stare at each other in awe.

When the soap is gone, she turns off the shower, and I grab us towels. A moment later, we're climbing into bed, dried and with towels wrapped around ourselves. As our backs rest against the headboard and our legs splay out in front of us, we sit in silence for a moment.

"You don't have to tell me what happened, but I need to know who I'm going to kill," she says.

I turn and face her. She really doesn't care to know the details. She's not begging to hear my trauma. Or to try to heal me, even though that shower alone went a long way toward healing me. She didn't coddle me. She laughed with me. She took care of me without making it too intimate.

"My punishment was not physical torture; my life was not threatened—I wasn't held down and raped." I look away, forcing myself to continue. I love her, and she deserves to know everything—one story at a time.

"But you've already figured that part out." I look back to her. She folds her legs to her chest and hugs herself, instinctually not touching me while I relive tonight.

"They sent me to a bar, where I was to meet a woman by

the name of Heather Truce. She's married to the leader of the Blackfire gang. They're a rival gang who stole a shipment of our weapons last year."

"Retribution is required," she whispers.

I nod. "My mission was simple—seduce her, take her back to the hotel room, and film myself fucking her in the dirtiest ways possible."

"Then send it to her husband."

I nod.

She reaches out, touching my hand softly, but I pull it back. She bites her lip and tucks her hand back around herself, realizing her mistake at once.

I wince. I don't want her to feel uncomfortable touching me, but I just can't handle it in this moment.

"You should hate me. I fucked another woman tonight. And then I let you suck my cock like I love you," I say.

"You do love me. You didn't want to fuck that woman."

"And yet I did fuck her!" I growl, panting. "I fucked her! Do you hear me? I fucked another woman."

She shakes her head, her eyes sharp with determination. "You were forced to sleep with her. You didn't want to."

"But I did..." my hands tremble, and my eyes water as I look at her. *They threatened to take turns raping Lilith if I didn't.* But I don't allow myself to say those words out loud.

"And even if this time was forced, I've willingly done it before."

I wait for her reaction, for her disgust to appear. But her face is just as determined as ever.

"I'm their whore, the man they send out to seduce and fuck others to get revenge, to get secrets. And I do it because I'm good at it. That's my role. I never fail at seducing a woman, and it's all I'm good at."

She shakes her head. "You're not a whore. And you are more than a good lay, so much more."

"Maybe, but that's why they won't kill me. That's why they took me back after I betrayed them with Lennox. That's why I'm Titus's number two. I'm their secret weapon who can fuck his way into getting information instead of having to steal it or go to war over it." My voice drips in shame.

"When...when did this start?"

"It's been this way for as long as I can remember."

"Before initiation age?"

"Yes," I cringe.

She grinds her teeth together, her hands fisting as she pounds into the bed in anger. Then she studies me closely. "Despite all they've done to you, it's not the reason you plot revenge with Gage, is it?"

"No, it's not the reason."

"Even though it's reason enough." She shakes her head. "You're so selfless, sunshine. You're a beautiful, kind, selfless man. That's why every woman you fuck falls for you, trusts you, and spills her secrets to you. Women can't help falling in love with you."

"I'm pretty sure it's because of my cock."

She rolls her eyes playfully before a serious expression falls across her face. "Then how did I fall in love with you before I tasted it?"

CHAPTER 24

Lilith

HAYES SUCKS IN A BREATH, like I just stabbed him instead of telling him I love him. I'm not sure if he thinks he's that unlovable or that me loving him will risk my life further.

"I love you, Hayes," I say, my voice full of emotion.

"How?" he whispers and clears his throat. "You shouldn't have fallen in love with me. You—"

I grab his face and kiss him hard, washing away any feelings of doubt on his part. The kiss is hungry and needy. Our tongues lash against each other, and the towels clinging to our bodies begin to slip as we roll toward each other.

Everything else fades away except him. For once, my mind isn't on revenge. It isn't on protecting my family. It isn't on anything but him.

For once, I'm not cursing every event in my life that I went through, because maybe it was leading me to him. Maybe the universe had some far bigger plan than I could have ever imagined. Maybe it was all leading to this moment, to finding this broken man. Between his brokenness and mine, we somehow might make a whole.

I have hope for the first time in forever that I can have a future worth living. Not one for my family, but for me.

He breaks the kiss, resting his forehead against mine as his thumb strokes my cheek, and his fingers grip my neck. We both pant hard into each other's mouths. We toy with the idea of taking everything from each other and giving nothing back. Damn, the consequences.

"Lilith, I have to tell you—"

"No," I stop him. "I don't care about anything you've done in the past. If you don't fuck me right now, I'm going to explode in frustration. The edging the Retribution Kings had you do to me is nothing compared to how I'll feel now if you deny me. The only thing that will damper this need is if you tell me you don't want to fuck me. That you need space after what happened tonight."

"God, no. I need you as badly as you need me. I'm going to die if I don't make you mine, but—"

"Then have me. I don't care what punishments we face. I don't care about the consequences. This isn't about anyone but us. Fuck me until we pass out from exhaustion. And then, when we wake, we can make plans for our future. Tonight, just make love to me."

My hooded eyes meet his ravenous ones. "Our future. I like the sound of that," he says.

He exhales slowly, his breath hot on my lips. "Forgive me," he whispers so softly I'm not even sure I heard him. There is nothing he needs my forgiveness for, though.

I'm begging for this.

I want this.

I'm sure he's more familiar with what the Retribution Kings will do if they find out, but being with him is worth any consequence.

And then he's on top of me, straddling me in his towel as his mouth kisses mine. I kiss him with everything I have as my arms wrap around his neck, terrified something is going to interrupt this moment and take him away from me.

His hand drags down the center of my body, finding the opening of my towel and peeling the cotton fabric away.

He leans up on his elbow, his gaze going over every inch of my bare skin.

"I want to lick every freckle until I've counted them all." He nudges at my neck, kissing the sensitive spot beneath my ear.

"One," he says.

His tongue inches down my neck, kissing another spot. "Two."

"That will take forever," I breathe in a raspy voice.

He grins. "Forever—that sounds like a perfect amount of time to spend with you."

My eyes heat, and hot desire curls in my stomach. The ache between my legs grows as I hook a leg around his, watching as the movement knocks the towel off his waist.

He growls, "Three."

"Ugh, this is torture." I buck my hips up, needing to feel his hard body between my legs.

He laughs at my reaction. "I thought you were patient."

"Not when it comes to you. I've spent my entire life being patient. It was an asset to keep my virginity, something I could use to gain money and safety for my family. I'm done being patient."

His smile drops. "Your family is taken care of, Lilith."

"I know. They have money."

"Not just money. I had my friend Lennox hide them away. They're safe. The Retribution Kings can't hurt them. Never again."

My eyes dash side to side, studying him to see if I heard him correctly. If I didn't fall in love with him before, I would have in this moment. "Thank you."

"Don't thank me."

I roll us over until I'm straddling him as I suffocate him with my kisses. All I feel is need, need, need.

I need him.

I'm going crazy waiting for him to enter me.

My hand reaches down between us until I find his cock. I need to know if he feels the same way or if he's stalling because he can't stand to fuck me right now. But he's hard and ready.

I look deep into his eyes. "This is your choice. Stop me if you aren't ready, if this needs to happen another night."

He shakes his head. "My heart wouldn't be able to beat tomorrow if I don't have you tonight."

I grin and then hesitate. I'm not sure how to do this, and a tiny bit of fear drips in. *Will it hurt? Will I be a terrible lover? Will—?*

"I love you, Lilith. I always will." He kisses me so tenderly that any self-doubt disappears with his kiss.

"I love you too."

His eyes darken into seductive orbs as he stares up at me.

"I'll never let another man hurt you again."

"I know."

"Even me."

I frown. "You've never hurt me."

He nods as his hands guide my hips over his cock. His tip rests at my soaked entrance. I'm so wet for him, so ready.

His eyes lock on mine as he waits for me to move the final inch.

I roll my hips, sinking down onto his cock, and gasp.

Holy fuck.

My body grasps onto him, tightening and filling in a way I've never experienced before. I grab onto his shoulders, my nails digging in, as I take him in.

He grins up at me like I'm the most beautiful woman he's ever seen. "Exquisite."

I blush. "I don't think I can take more of you."

He chuckles deeply. With how self-sacrificing he is, he wouldn't force the issue. He'd do anything to make this pleasurable for me at the expense of his own pleasure.

"Kiss me," he says gently.

I lean down, his tongue licking over my lip before slipping into my mouth. At the same time, I feel him gently rock his hips up, and his cock pushes deeper inside me.

There's a stretching pain, but his kisses distract me as more of my wetness soaks him until the pain disappears completely.

But he's still not all the way inside me.

I slam my hips down.

He bites my bottom lip, and fullness rolls through my body. I feel him in every crevice of my body.

Neither of us moves, giving me time to adjust to the sensation. My tissues need time to stretch while he peppers me with kisses. A moment later, my body starts rocking up and down on its own accord.

"Fuck, Lilith. You feel incredible."

His voice is thick with desire.

"And you feel—god, like I'm never going to get enough. Like I'll never be able to leave this bed again."

"Good. I don't plan on leaving this bed except to make sure you're fed."

I nibble on his bottom lip. "I could live off of you. All I need is you."

"And I you."

Our hips rock faster against each other. My breasts grow heavy under his gaze as his hands rest on my hips. He leans up, his mouth capturing a nipple and swirling his tongue over the hardened tip. I almost come right then.

"Hayes," I gasp.

"I love my name on your lips."

"Hayes," I say again as I roll my hips up and down his cock. His piercing hits against my G-spot as I do, intensifying everything.

"Does your piercing give you pleasure?" I ask.

He licks his bottom lip, rocking into me in faster thrusts that leave me breathless, only allowing small whimpers to escape my throat.

"It brings you pleasure, and that brings me more pleasure than anything else."

He slows for a second as I lower my body over his so I can kiss him again. "So selfless."

"So worth it," he says as I pant over him.

We rock together, his cock slipping in and out. A cascade of feelings floods through my body. I've never experienced anything like this. It's so much more than having his tongue on me, so much more.

His thumb slips between my legs, rubbing over my clit, and I see stars. I grip onto him for dear life as my orgasm takes hold of me. My body shatters around him.

"Hayes," I cry into his shoulder, my teeth sinking into his flesh.

A second later, his warm cum fills me as he growls into my hair.

Our orgasms rock through us, until I collapse on top of him, exhausted.

My eyes drift close as pleasure fills every dark corner of my body, pushing out the pain of my past.

"I love you," he whispers, stroking my hair.

"I love you, too." I wrap my arms around him.

"Tell me everything, everything you're feeling. I want to know it all," he says.

"I'm thinking that was the most incredible thing I've

ever experienced. I didn't know it could be like that. I didn't know I could ever love like this again."

"Same."

He grins into my hair.

"I'm thinking I trust you with everything. My body, my family, my secrets. You've given me so much; all I care about now is you and finding the man who killed my father."

Hayes tenses. "You don't know who killed your father?"

"No," I shake my head. "I don't know who ordered it or who pulled the trigger. Usually, Retribution Kings are quite proud of their kills. So there's something strange about my father's murder."

I shiver, and Hayes looks down at us. I follow his gaze to our sticky cum tinted with my blood.

"Let me get something to clean you up," he says.

I groan in protest as he rolls me off him to head to the bathroom. But I can't help smiling like a fool. And a fool I am for thinking that fucking and loving Hayes fixed everything.

"Hello, Lilith," a deep voice says from the shadows of the room.

I freeze, my eyes darting to the man walking toward the bed.

Hayes reappears in the bathroom door and stops dead in his tracks as he spots the man.

The man steps forward toward the end of the bed until I can make out who it is.

"Well done, Hayes. You did your job well. But I can take it from here," Titus says.

CHAPTER 25

Lilith

"JOB? What job? What are you talking about?" I ask, looking from Titus to Hayes as I yank one of the discarded towels over my body.

Hayes is standing stark naked in the doorway, looking at Titus. He no longer has eyes for me.

"Thank you. I did my job as promised," Hayes says.

What the fuck?

My eyes burn into the side of Hayes's head, but no matter how I stare, he won't look at me.

"Hayes? What is Titus talking about?" my voice trembles.

I know—deep down, I know. But I can't accept the crazy thoughts spinning in my head. I must be wrong. There has to be an easy explanation for all of this. My world can't be crumbling apart right now.

"I'm so sorry, Lilith. I'm so fucking sorry for everything you had to endure, but I had no choice. You're the right woman for the job, and you had to go through a trial," Titus says.

My head snaps in his direction as I narrow my eyes. I

replay his words in my head, but they don't make any sense. *What is he talking about?*

Titus takes a step toward me with his warm brown eyes, thick black hair, and kind smile.

I scramble to the top of the bed and scrunch my knees up to my chest, like prey cornered by a predator.

Titus stops when he sees the fear in my eyes.

"I'm sorry, I know you fear me. After everything you've endured, you have every right to. But I'm hoping with time, you'll learn to trust me, like me, and maybe eventually love me."

I shake my head. "If you want any of those things, you'll walk out the door right now and let Hayes and I talk."

Titus sighs as he looks to Hayes. "Do you want to explain or shall I?"

Hayes looks at me briefly out of the corner of his eyes. "You better do it."

My mouth falls. Hayes won't even talk to me.

"Hayes is the best we have in the Retribution Kings, the absolute best. And I trust him with my life," Titus begins.

Hayes leans against the doorframe, looking bored with this conversation. If he's feeling anything else, I can't tell. So I turn to Titus, hoping to make some sense out of this.

"When I selected you, Lilith, I knew the rest of the Retribution Kings would want proof that you were the right choice. You would need to be tested. Your true loyalties would need to be revealed, especially after what happened to your father. They would want proof that you weren't working with one of our enemies."

What did Hayes tell him?

I glare at Hayes, but he still won't look at me.

"And what did you find out, Hayes?" Titus asks.

"Lilith is loyal. She isn't working for an enemy. She only

cares about getting revenge for her father's death," Hayes answers.

While shooting daggers in Hayes's direction, I grind my teeth together so hard I'm pretty sure I broke one. He won't answer any of my questions, but he'll answer Titus. *Really?*

I turn back to Titus, feeling the need to clarify my goals.

"I want revenge for my father. I want to take down the entire Retribution Kings for what happened to him. And since you're the head of the Retribution Kings, that makes me the opposite of loyal."

Titus chuckles. "You are a fiery one, just as Hayes said."

I hold my gaze on Titus, glaring at him with everything I have. Hopefully, there's a weapon nearby to threaten him with.

"I'm sorry Hayes had to seduce you and fuck you in order to get the information from you. We had to be sure you were telling the truth. But I'm sure fucking Hayes wasn't a hardship. I've heard he's a great lover."

My eyes widen, and my cheeks pink, but Hayes doesn't react at all.

He just told me he was their whore. He told me all about how he's paraded about to fuck women to gain their secrets. He said he always succeeds.

My heart shutters in my chest.

Was it all a game?

Was none of it real?

Did he not really love me?

Was he just trying to seduce me because Titus told him to?

Is he loyal to the Retribution Kings? To Titus?

I have no idea what's true and what's an act.

Titus's face falls slightly, seemingly feeling sorry for me. *Great.*

I clear my throat and shake off my emotions, becoming as emotionless as Hayes. I will not let either of these men see me. I may be losing whatever game these two are playing, but it doesn't mean I won't find a way to win in the end.

Titus nods at me with a soft smile. "I knew you were strong. I knew I chose well. I just hope you'll agree to choose me in return."

My stomach drops as I suspect what he's asking me.

"And what exactly does choosing you mean?"

"Marrying me," Titus says.

CHAPTER 26

Lilith

IT'S BEEN three weeks since I learned the truth. Three weeks since Titus took me from Hayes and brought me to his mansion, my gilded cage. Three weeks since I've seen Hayes.

Still, I don't have any more answers than I did three weeks ago.

I'm losing my mind waiting for answers, waiting for Hayes to come kidnap me and tell me he was fooling Titus, not me. But with every day that passes, that hope begins to vanish.

I'm a prisoner here, although no one has said it. No one has told me I can't leave, and yet, I haven't stepped foot beyond the back terrace in three weeks. Bodyguards constantly follow me, and I'm never left alone.

On the second day, Gage was one of my guards. I thought that was the day I would finally get answers. But Gage managed to not speak a single word to me during his entire twelve-hour shift.

I expected Hayes to come that night. Maybe Gage was

guarding me so he could tell Hayes how to get me out. But he didn't come.

I'm on my own.

The only real human interaction I have is dinner with Titus every night. And while he's tried to engage me in polite conversation, he hasn't offered any more details about Hayes. He hasn't spoken of us getting married. He hasn't even made a move on me. Not a hug, a kiss, an inappropriate touch—nothing.

I'm stuck in this perpetual loop of doing nothing, waiting for answers and getting none, and not knowing what my future holds. I'm not even sure if Titus still wants to marry me. Maybe after getting to know me, he regrets his choice. Or maybe he thinks I'll slit his throat in his sleep.

I haven't made a violent move toward anyone. I've been biding my time, not sure if Hayes revealed my fighting skills to them or not. If he didn't, then surprise is on my side. I've waited long enough for Hayes, so it's up to me. I'm going to figure out the truth one way or another, even if I end up dead for it.

I walk down the long hallway with two guards in front of me and two behind me, like I'm in some maximum security prison. Titus knows, I realize. He knows I'm a threat, and I could escape if I wanted to. That's the only explanation for so many men guarding me—it's about keeping me from attacking them.

Hayes told him every one of my secrets. He truly betrayed me in every way possible.

I scowl as I stomp to the dining room, wearing a long floral sundress. It's far too cheery for me, but it is good for one thing: concealing weapons.

I've gathered three knives and one gun in the weeks I've spent here. They're strapped to my thighs, ready to use.

"Good evening, Lilith. I've missed you. I hope you had a

relaxing day," Titus says as I enter the dining room. He stands from the table to greet me.

"It's been as relaxing as any other prison, I suppose."

He chuckles at that. "I'm sorry about that. As soon as we're married, you'll have all the freedoms you desire."

My eyebrows raise. "So I won't have bodyguards?"

Titus's smile drops. "Everything is negotiable. I would prefer you to be safe, but ultimately, the decision will be yours."

"So if I choose not to marry you?"

He sighs, running his hand through his thick strands. "Then we won't be married. I hope I can change your mind, but I won't force you to do anything you don't want to do."

I study him, hating his answer. I see the confidence in his eyes. He truly thinks I'll agree to marry him.

"Fine," I stomp past him to my chair and take a seat before he or his guards can slide out the chair for me. "Then I want to negotiate now, *alone*."

My gaze scans across the four guards standing in each corner of the room, and I wait to see what Titus will do.

"Leave us. You all have the rest of the night off," Titus says as he takes a seat across the circular table from me. Now we sit alone, not more than five feet away, staring each other down. We're each confident in a looming victory, but one of us will be sorely disappointed.

He smiles at me.

I glare back.

"I love that you don't smile often. You make me earn it," he says.

"I don't recall ever having smiled because of something you did."

"No, but you will. Once you mend your heart." He sighs as he lifts his red wine to his lips and sinks deeper into his chair. "I made a mistake by sending Hayes. He's too good at his job, and it's going to take longer for you to get over him than I first thought."

"I'm over him," I snap back.

"Of course." Titus smiles slyly. "I only meant that the betrayal must have stung. And it is, after all, a reflection on me, since I was the one who gave him the mission."

"It would only be a betrayal if I fell for him, and I regretted it. But as you said, the sex was good, so I have no regrets."

"Good."

"What I don't understand is how you're not bothered by one of your men fucking me if you truly want to marry me?"

"It was unfortunate. But then again, fucking a virgin isn't really my thing. You deserved to have lived before being tied down to me."

Titus is charming and good-looking. If he wasn't the current leader of the Retribution Kings, and if I weren't hung up on a man who betrayed me, I would give him a chance.

A daring look crosses his face. "So tell me, where should we start the negotiations?"

I take a deep breath. It's now or never. I hike my dress up under the table until I have a grip on two of my knives.

In and out.

On the next exhale, I strike, throwing a blade hard at Titus's shoulder. As soon as the blade leaves my hand, I'm out of my chair, knocking it backward as I slide across the table. With the second knife in my hand, I land on Titus, who is pinned to his chair by my first knife.

We fall back with the chair, and I press the knife to his throat as I straddle him. I expect him to grab his own weapon or to call a guard to help him. I don't believe he truly dismissed all the guards, or we're not being surveilled.

A wicked grin crosses his lips as his eyes light up. It's not the expression I was expecting from a man trapped and threatened with knives. I could slice his carotid at any moment, and yet he smiles.

"Well done. You are just as Hayes said you were. I've been waiting for three weeks for you to show your skills. It's just as incredible as I imagined."

I scowl at him. "I could kill you. I'd wipe that smirk off your face and treat me with respect if I were you."

He swallows gently, his eyes darting to my hand as if he's just realized the blade is real and not made of wood. "I know you could kill me. But every man in my house could kill me at any moment. My enemies could attack and kill me. I could die getting hit by the bus crossing the street. Death isn't something I fear or a new concept to me. It's something I live with every day of my life." He pauses. "What is new is that you have the skills to be able to kill me. Skills that, if Hayes is to be believed, you taught yourself?"

I nod.

"Impressive. You're incredibly impressive."

He's charming, but he's not Hayes. He's not the one my heart aches for.

"Take me to Hayes. Let me have a private conversation with him."

His lips rise ever so slightly. "All you had to do was ask. You didn't have to threaten to kill me. If you want to see Hayes or any other person, you're free to."

I frown. "Without your guards."

"As I said, everything is up for negotiation. The guards will take you to him, and then they can stay outside while you talk. Fair enough?"

"Fine," I growl, pressing the knife to his neck until a bead of blood appears.

He doesn't flinch. As the leader of the Retribution Kings, he's used to pain.

"Now, ask me for something real. Something you don't think I'll give you."

I narrow my eyes at him, not understanding.

"Ask me," he says.

"Tell me who killed my father. Help me get revenge on all who took part in his death. And maybe I won't kill you."

He shrugs. "I have no doubt you'll kill me if I piss you off enough. Good thing I don't plan on doing that."

"We'll see about that."

"I didn't kill your father. And I didn't order him to be killed. I wasn't in a position of power when he died."

I believe him. I never really thought he killed him or had anything to do with his death. But I'm sure Titus has killed plenty of innocent people.

"But I do know who killed your father. I know who was behind his death, and I will help you get revenge—if you agree to marry me."

I narrow my eyes at him. "Help me first; then I'll consider marrying you."

"Of course."

"You'll help me, even if it compromises your position as leader of the Retribution Kings?"

"I will."

I don't trust him, but I don't have another choice.

He grabs my wrist. "Do we have an agreement?"

He squeezes, forcing me to drop the knife.

"After I speak to Hayes, I'll give you my answer," I hiss. I need to hear what that lying bastard has to say first.

CHAPTER 27

Lilith

OF COURSE, Hayes is at a club. I stare through the crowd with Titus at my side. His guards stayed outside the front door, and he agreed to leave as soon as I'm with Hayes.

Titus said Hayes would protect me, which is probably true. *But who will protect him?*

"There he is," Titus says, pointing to the dance floor.

I scrunch my nose in disgust as I see him dancing with a red-haired woman in leather pants and a crop top. She's gorgeous and a great dancer. Their hips move in unison to the music.

He grins at her with one of his signature smiles, showing off all his pearly white teeth and adorable dimple. She bites her lip hungrily in response.

He leans in, whispering something in her ear, before tucking a strand of hair behind her ear. He kisses her jawline sweetly and then moves swiftly to her lips—capturing them in one hungry kiss.

I can't watch. And yet, I can't tear my eyes away, either.

"I'm sorry. This must be hard on you. I'm here as a friend if you need me," Titus says.

"This isn't hard. And you aren't my friend."

"Soon to be husband, then?"

My fists tense at my sides. "Only as a means to an end. I will never like you, never fall for you, and definitely never love you." Even if he turned out to be the greatest man on the planet, I would never allow myself to love him. I can't, not after the hole in my chest Hayes left. I'll never allow that weakness to enter my body again.

"Are you good? Or do you want me to stay?" Titus asks in response.

"Go," I say, my eyes locked on Hayes as I begin to strut toward him. I don't notice if Titus keeps to his word and leaves or not; I don't care.

I stomp toward Hayes, not sure what I'm going to do until I'm upon him. Upon reaching him, I yank his arm and pull him free from her. With my other hand, I slap him hard across the cheek.

It's not enough, not nearly enough to stifle my rage. But I'll save stabbing him for when we are in a more private place.

"Leave us," I say to the woman.

She stares wide-eyed, clinging onto Hayes's arm.

Hayes finally looks at me with his big green eyes. There's a flash of shock, and then amusement settles into his gaze. He pulls a hotel room key from his wallet and hands it to the woman.

"Room 302. I'll meet you there later, Ruby."

Ruby—the woman he mistook me for. This is her—another mark, another mission, just like I was.

She smirks at me and then struts off with his hotel room key in her hand.

"What do you want, Lilith?" He cocks his head in that annoying way he does.

I want you. "I want to talk to you privately."

He holds out his arms like we can talk here in the middle of a crowded and loud dance floor.

I roll my eyes and yank him off the floor behind me. I keep walking until I find a booth in a far corner of the club, and we both drop into opposite sides. This will have to do. There is nowhere else more private. And if we are actually alone together, I'll either kiss him or kill him. Neither of those options sounds like a good idea at the moment.

"What's wrong? You're soon to be hubby not making you happy?" He's smiling, fucking smiling at me like nothing happened, and this is all a game.

I reach for the dagger at my hip but stop. Violence isn't going to get me anywhere with him. He knows I won't kill him. I'll just make him bleed, and it won't make him talk or tell the truth.

I don't say anything. I just study him, trying to figure him out, trying to figure the truth out.

Is it an act? A game?

Who is he loyal to?

Is he just a weapon?

Or is he forced to play this role as a punishment?

Is he protecting me?

Does he love me?

I can't make sense of him.

But when I look at him, I hear him say *I love you, Lilith, Lily, murderous one*. I see him smile in my mind—one that truly reaches his eyes and isn't forced. I feel the pull to him. The attraction. The way he kissed me, touched me, fucked me.

It had to be real.

It couldn't be fake.

"You can stop the act now. We're alone. Titus and his men are outside. He knows his only chance of me agreeing to marry him is if this conversation is truly private. Talk to me. Tell me your plan," I demand.

His eyebrows slowly raise, and he leans back in the booth, resting his arm across the back as if he doesn't have a care in the world.

"Oh, you think I'm acting? You think I have a plan?"

"I do," I reply.

"You're wrong."

"I know you love me."

He laughs. It's a vicious, cruel laugh—an act to push me away. *But why?*

"Ask Ruby if I love her. She'd say the same thing. I'm sorry, but it's an act. You got played, and I'm sorry for that, but the game is over. You lost. Move on."

I frown, not sure how to break him.

"You aren't going to save me?" I ask.

He narrows his gaze and leans onto his forearms on the table so his lips are close to mine. "You don't need saving. Titus is a good man. He won't hurt you. He won't even force you to marry him. It will be your choice."

I shake my head. "I don't believe you. I'm not giving up on you, not yet. Titus agreed to help me get revenge and help me find the man who killed my father. I promised I'd marry him if he did. And I won't back out of that promise. So if you want me, if you have some plan, you better do it quick."

Hayes tenses ever so slightly. Most people wouldn't notice, but I know him well enough to notice the change.

I frown.

"You had a secret you were going to tell me. I know you're hiding something. What is it?"

I don't expect him to answer me. I don't expect him to tell me anything, but there's a wicked smirk on his lips.

"I don't have a plan to save you, but I should probably kill you before you kill me."

"And why would I kill you?"

"Because I killed your father."

No.

No.

No.

No.

He couldn't have, *but why would he lie?* He has no reason to hide it, not when Titus agreed to help me get revenge.

The man I love killed my father. My heart shatters into a million pieces, and now I know I'll never recover. But I don't let him see my brokenness, so I stare him down until I'm able to respond.

"Then I guess we'll see who kills whom first."

———

Thank you for reading Hayes & Lilith's story! I hope you enjoyed it! There story concludes in LILITH coming in November

Want to start reading Lilith before November? You can start reading Lilith now on my Patreon.

Hayes killed my father.
He's my enemy, not my friend.
Not the man I fell in love with.
He's a fraud.
Now, I must marry another.
A man who can truly help me get revenge.
Together we will kill Hayes.
We will get retribution.
And I'll find a way to get my heart back from Hayes.

Pre-Order Lilith

JOIN ELLA'S NEWSLETTER & NEVER MISS A SALE
OR NEW RELEASE → ellamiles.com/freebooks

Also by Ella Miles

TRUTH OR LIES:

Taken by Lies #1

Betrayed by Truths #2

Trapped by Lies #3

Stolen by Truths #4

Possessed by Lies #5

Consumed by Truths #6

SINFUL TRUTHS:

Sinful Truth #1

Twisted Vow #2

Reckless Fall #3

Tangled Promise #4

Fallen Love #5

Broken Anchor #6

LIES SERIES:

Lies We Share: A Prologue #0.5

Vicious Lies #1

Desperate Lies #2

Fated Lies #3

Cruel Lies #4

Dangerous Lies #5

Endless Lies #6

RETRIBUTION GAMES SERIES:

Mistaken Hero #1

Forbidden Princess #2

Tempted Hero #3

Fatal Princess #4

Tortured Hero #5

Dangerous Princess #6

RETRIBUTION KINGS SERIES:

Lennox #1

PRETEND SERIES:

Pretend I'm Yours

Pretend We're Over

Pretend: The Complete Series

DIRTY SERIES:

Dirty Obsession

Dirty Addiction

Dirty Revenge

Dirty: The Complete Series

ALIGNED SERIES:

Aligned: Volume 1

Aligned: Volume 2

Aligned: Volume 3

Aligned: Volume 4

Aligned: The Complete Series Boxset

UNFORGIVABLE SERIES:

Heart of a Thief

Heart of a Liar

Heart of a Prick

Unforgivable: The Complete Series Boxset

MAYBE, DEFINITELY SERIES:

Maybe Yes

Maybe Never

Maybe Always

Maybe: The Complete Series

Definitely Yes

Definitely No

Definitely Forever

Definitely: The Complete Series

STANDALONES:

Finding Perfect

Savage Love

Too Much

Not Sorry

Hate Me or Love Me: An Enemies to Lovers Romance Collection

About the Author

Ella Miles writes steamy romance, including everything from dark suspense romance that will leave you on the edge of your seat to contemporary romance that will leave you laughing out loud or crying. Most importantly, she wants you to feel everything her characters feel as you read.

Ella is currently living her own happily ever after near the Rocky Mountains with her high school sweetheart husband. Her heart is also taken by her goofy five year old black lab who is scared of everything, including her own shadow.

Ella is a USA Today Bestselling Author & Top 50 Bestselling Author.

Stalk Ella at:
www.ellamiles.com
ella@ellamiles.com

www.ingramcontent.com/pod-product-compliance
Lightning Source LLC
Chambersburg PA
CBHW061442210726
48287CB00007B/2326